Take One More Chance

Take One More Chance

A satire comedy by a sixteen-year old

Shriya Garg

MP

MAHAVEER PUBLISHERS

Published by
MAHAVEER PUBLISHERS
4764/2A, 23-Ansari Road, Daryaganj
New Delhi – 110002
Ph. : 011 – 66629669–79–89
011 – 23244999
e-mail : mahaveerpublishers@gmail.com

© Shriya Garg

First Published: January 2011
Third Impression: February 2012

Take One More Chance
ISBN (10) : 8183520146
ISBN (13) : 9788183520140

Distributed by
VAIBHAV BOOK SERVICE
e-mail : vaibhavbookservice@gmail.com

Distributed in Nepal by
BAJRANGBALI BOOK ENTERPRISES PVT. LTD.
Jyatha Mushyabahal, Ward No. 27, Kathmandu, Nepal
e-mail : bajrangbalibooks@gmail.com

Printed by Jaico Printers, New Delhi

Dedications

For my family
and for my friends.
Thank you for always being there.

Acknowledgement

Writing is said to be an isolated business. Personally, nothing could be farther away from the truth as my list of names would prove to you.

The biggest thank you would be to my sisters Riya and Aastha. I don't think this book would have existed if not for them. They laughed at all the right places (not to mention the wrong ones) and were there even when I could have killed for an hour of solitude, but you get what I mean.

Another thank you would go to my brother, who in his own annoying way helped me a lot with *Take One More Chance*. Whenever I wanted information on how to kill off or mutate a character, he always gave the best idea.

For my Mom, a writer herself, who made me what I am today. You are the best Ma, even though I do not always believe it myself.

To the rest of my family – Dad, Aunt Anuradha, Uncle Sandeep, grandmother and grandfather, for their curiosity about my book and the money I would make *if* it got published. (Did you notice the *if*?)

Then, of course my friends, who made my life beautiful by just being in it and whose interests kept this book going: Akanksha, Damodar, Nishith, Piyush, Ritwik, Saurabh, Sugandha and Vandana. Even if we don't always stay in touch, most of my best memories while growing up include you and nothing would change that.

Thank you, everyone at Mahaveer for giving me this opportunity. Also, thank you, Marina, Holly and Mariam for your contribution.

And last but never the least, a special thank you to Ritwik for the title and for giving me advice even when I didn't want it.

A Word or Two

"Books have to be heavy, because they carry the whole world with them."

—Cornelia Funke

Prologue

9:30 p.m.

It is a truth, universally acknowledged, that a single man in possession of a good fortune must be in want of a wife.

Not the best beginning, I accept. In fact, it is downright clichéd, borrowed and old, *but,* that doesn't make it any less *true*. Moreover, it is very appropriate as the beginning of my suicide novel.

A suicide *novel?*

You see, everybody has heard of suicide notes, but I have always been a little different. So, when I started with my suicide note, I realised that a single page was not close enough to the list of grievances that this cruel world has caused me.

Thus, after much deliberation and consideration, I decided that to maximise my parents' guilt and suffering and make my brother and sisters realise their offences against me, I should write a whole novel.

I am going to start my story from the beginning, so that the said people can see how unjust they've been to me all the while.

I am Naina Kashyap, a 25-year-old accountant who has also completed her Masters in business administration and works in the finance department of an accounting firm in New Delhi.

I live with this huge, boisterous family that comprises my 22-year-old younger sister Ria, then my cousins Shaurya (24) and Manya (23) and myself. Shaurya and Manya's father is my father's younger brother.

Since all of us are of almost the same age group, we never cease bickering and fighting and have also spent many memorable holidays together. Till the past three days, I would have believed what the others thought of us all – a very close-knit extended family. But then something happened that made me realise how cleverly they had been deceiving me since the past 25 years. Come to think of it, since Ria is only 22-years old, she could not have deceived me for 25 years and the same holds true for Shaurya and Manya as well.

Coming to my parents – Jai Kashyap and Shivani Kashyap, that is, Dad and Mom – they are a national disaster. It is said that most marriages are made in heaven. If so, then theirs is a pact signed by the devil in the reddest, hottest and deepest pits of hell.

To present a living example, think of Rahul Gandhi – nice, handsome, charming and someone who has devoted his life to the greater good of the nation; on the other hand, however, you take Mallika Sherawat, the bold, seductive actress of Bollywood.

Can you imagine what would happen if Rahul Gandhi married Mallika Sherawat? Dad and Mom are like that. Though both of them are really nice in their own place, but a marriage between them would surely spell disaster. It would be the battlefield of Kargil, which our residence is. Luckily enough, Uncle Prakash, Dad's younger brother and my Aunt Nandini are a pretty compatible couple. Comparatively. Their household runs smoothly except when Shaurya is around as he is the hell-raiser in the family. But, less than me, of course. I often think that because Manya had such an older brother, she made a brilliant cop.

10:30 p.m.
Sorry for breaking off so abruptly. An old friend of Dad came for dinner due to which I had to be around to serve him water and snacks. After all, I am the eldest daughter and everything.

Shriya Garg

Honestly, one cannot even write a suicide novel in peace these days. What has the world come to?

Where was I? Yeah, introducing my family. I am done with everybody except myself. This goes to prove I am not the self-centred witch people think I am. I am Naina Kashyap, an unnaturally sharp girl with an opinion about everything. However, it is not my fault that nobody wants to listen to my opinions.

Neither is my sense of humour shared by many. I remember during my school days, teachers would glare at me when I made a wisecrack. I can vividly remember the first time it happened. The art teacher was giving us a lecture on creativity and how some parents can suppress a child's creativity. At that time, I was a fresh faced, 12-year old girl.

"When you give a two-year old some mountains and rivers to colour," Miss Daisy was saying, "what does a teacher say when she sees how the child has coloured it? Does she criticise the young child for colouring the sky green and the trees blue? Tell me, what would she say?"

"Do you suffer from colour blindness?" the innocent 12-year-old in me didn't realise that it was a rhetorical question and hence the reply.

The teacher continued speaking as if I hadn't interrupted.

Sadly, this wasn't the only incident when my teacher glared at me. I was often shouted upon by my classmates.

I also remember the time when a girl of Class XI started bawling on learning that I was going to be sent to her section. She was *that* terrified of me.

Thank God, my best friend is different. Vandana Sinha is everything I am not. She is shy and an introvert. She hates getting into fights and looks so fragile that automatically a man wants to protect her from the cockroaches and lizards of the world. She is one of those pretty elementary school teachers who especially cater to the kids of the elite of Delhi. Vandana loves her job and is perfect wife material. She is a true romantic by nature and has dreamt of her marriage since she was a kid. Once she confided to me that she had even visualised the dress she would wear if she married a man from a religion different to hers. What if she married a South Indian or a Christian or a North Indian? Three cases would call for a different wedding trousseau and she has fantasised in great detail about each of them.

Coming to the present, though she rarely loses her cool, her temper is legendary. In the 15 years that I've known her, she has lost her temper only twice. The first time was when she was 15-year old and had slapped her maths teacher across his face because he refused to answer one of her inane questions, and the second when, as an 18-year old, she pushed a college senior, who was ragging her, into the 15-feet deep swimming pool. Thank God for the lifeguard who was nearby.

Thus, Vandana was the perfect best friend material for me. Every tall girl needs a short best friend and everything.

We became friends when I first defended her against a school bully in Class IX. Since then, I've always harboured a protective streak towards her. I have observed that men tend to take advantage of her because she is small and frail and I am her only shield between her and the cruel world. But despite that, I would give up a lung to exchange places with her.

In high school, boys used to smile on seeing her and fight to pay for her coffee but when they saw the tall giant standing next to her watch them like a hawk – yours truly – their smiles would disappear and they would stealthily slip away.

This is why I am often asked this question, "Who in the right mind made you an accountant?"

The answer to that is that it was my father. He wanted a respectable career for me and when he found that his daughter had no interest in science, he pushed me into commerce.

At times even my brother dreads entering into a verbal duel with me.

"I wish that some day I could take you to court with me," he'd say with a faraway look. "It would be the quickest case to be ever won in history."

He obviously meant it sarcastically.

Shaurya is a lawyer by the way and is employed with a private law firm in Gurgaon.

Enough of that. Let us come to the real reasons for this suicide novel. I am thinking of listing them so as to make my pathetic existence seem even more pathetic.

List #1: Reasons for Naina Kashyap's Pathetic Existence

- She has a job which she hates because she is a creative and imaginative person by nature and there is nothing creative and/or imaginative in numbers.
- Her boss makes a pass at everyone in the department, except her. She doesn't know whether to be relieved or be annoyed.
- Despite being 25-years old, she has never been in a steady relationship. While Vandana made the college jocks drool, Naina makes them wince.
- Her parents hate each other and do not sleep in the same room. Yet, they pretend they are a big, happy family which could make even a woman who is not pregnant nauseous.
- She is writing a book which never seems to end. Whenever she thinks she has completed the final draft, she gets a new idea to twist the story in another direction, which forces her to start all over again.

You see now *how* awful it is! You would be surprised to learn that I totally flipped out that day six months ago.

"Marriage? Me? What the f – Dad? Are you crazy?"

Dad remains unfazed by my reaction, "Yes, Naina. Marriage. Yours, and for the record, no, I am not crazy."

As always, when my father's strange sense of humour surfaces, I ignore it.

"Dad, but what, *why*? Mom!" I stutter and then shriek. We are having this family discussion in the dining room and all four of us, Mom, Dad, Uncle Prakash and Aunt Nandini, are seated in a circle around the table.

"Listen to what he has to say, sweetheart," Mom says. "I know he rarely says something that is worth listening, but – "

"Shivani…" Uncle Prakash warns Mom and she makes a face and continues, "– but that doesn't mean what he is saying is unimportant. This is about your future, honey."

I believe that Rahul Gandhi would agree to marry Mallika Sherawat only when Pakistan drops a hydrogen bomb on Mumbai, but apparently there is one more point when they would be in agreement: Naina Kashyap's marriage.

Ria and Shaurya watch the unfolding drama with amusement. Manya, who is the most serious among us all, observes everything but her expression reveals nothing.

"Naina, you are 25-years old. You have completed your higher education; you have a steady job and all your friends are now getting married. Matrimony is the next obvious step for you as well."

"Vandana gets engaged every month!" I defend myself. "You make me sound as if I am a baby-making machine put on earth for use by the holy species called males. This is the twenty-first century Dad. Today women deliver more than just babies.

"Hear, hear," Ria cheers but falls quiet when I shoot her my best frosty glare.

It seems that my infamous quick wit seems to have forgotten its existence when faced with such mind-numbing shock.

"Yes, Naina. Really," Aunt Nandini intervenes, "there is no reason for you to be so surprised at this."

"Your elders are right," Uncle Prakash adds.

This is a conspiracy. And I realise that.

"I think I know the reason." He glances at me suspiciously before adding, "Is there anybody special in your life?"

"Special? Oh, no!" I reply, mortified. I don't want my whole family to know that I've been single for every one of these past 25 Valentine's Days.

"No, no, sweetie, it is okay. You can tell us if there is really someone special in your life. We have, ah, no problem. We would love to meet him."

I concentrate on my shoes so that I don't have to look at them. "Mom, really, there is no one. No need to rub your nose into it."

Dad clears his throat and says, "I know today's children are very modern. They don't believe in uh, keeping themselves, no, saving themselves for their marriage beds, and..."

"Omigosh, Dad!" I scream as Ria giggles and discreetly excuses herself.

"And so," he continues, despite the whole family's discomfort, "we would really like to meet your young man. You need to be frank with us, Naina. If we find him acceptable..."

Even Shaurya holds up his cell phone and says, "Emergency," and sneaks out of the room.

"I hate you guys," I scream after him and add, "Dad there is *no one*."

"Naina," he looks at me over his spectacles, "please, be honest with us."

"Dad, think about it," I cut him short, "*who* would be crazy enough to willingly fall for me?"

Dad pauses for a second and then his expression clears. "Well, that's that," he concludes.

I am a bit peeved to see him accept the explanation so promptly but I do not say anything.

"Then what is the problem?"

I look around from one serious face to the next before saying, "I don't think I am ready for marriage and kids. Honestly, can you see me holding a child in my lap and singing him to sleep?"

Manya sniggers at the picture I paint because the thought is *that* ridiculous.

"Marriage does not mean children," Uncle Prakash says.

I snort, "In India, it does."

"If you go with this attitude, young lady, then you'll never be ready to settle down. Already people are talking about you. A 25-year old, pretty female sitting at home? It does not bode well for our status in society."

"I hardly sit at home," I point out, but my logic is ignored. I am outnumbered. There is no hope.

"At least meet a few young men," Dad insists. "What is the harm?"

Oh no. It is as if history is repeating itself. In Class XI, when we had to choose our individual streams, my father pushed me into science, because he wanted to make his oldest daughter an engineer. At that time, I wanted to become a journalist. He'd replied that it wasn't a worthy profession and that I could write even after completing my engineering course and M.B.A. But till then, I had to devote eight years of my life to science.

We had fought. I'd thrown tantrums. In the end we'd reached a compromise. I'd go in for commerce instead of humanities as I'd originally wanted to and thus become an accountant. It was a respectable job as well as financially secure, unlike a journalist's – at least according to my father.

I am ready to fight, I vow. I am not going to budge an inch. No matter what happens, I am not going to let my naïve parents destroy my life like they did theirs. So as to satisfy their parents' wishes, each married a partner whom each thoroughly disliked from the beginning. I am not going to fall in that trap. I am not, I am not.

I am not.

"So, you're getting married?" Vandana asks as soon as I enter her bedroom and collapse on the bed.

"Did you hear a word of what I said last night?" I snap.

"Yes, yes, I did. But despite the truce which you made with your father of waiting for six months for Mr Right to come along, there is no denying the fact that there is going to be a marriage." She sighs, "Wow, you're *so* lucky."

I cup my chin in misery, "What is the chance of my Mr Right coming along in the next six months when he hasn't even made an appearance in my dreams for the past 25 years?"

"I have been thinking about it all night..." she begins. "And the answer is obvious."

I am immediately wary.

"What?"

"Promise me you'd hear me out first."

I think about it for a moment, "Okay."

"We are going man hunting!"

"We are what?"

"Man hunting. The main plot of a dozen beautiful romance novels," she sighs dreamily. "It is so perfect."

"Hold on, hold on, rein in your thoughts. What are you talking about?"

She is so excited that she can't keep still. Getting up, she fetches a pen and a paper, "Come on, we are going to draw up a list."

"What list? I shake my head. "Vandana, what are you talking about?"

"Look over here."

List #2: Qualities Naina Kashyap's Mr Right Would/Should Have

1) Vandana: A good **sense of humour**.

Naina: But it should be dry. He shouldn't guffaw at his own jokes. That is a big no-no.

2) Vandana: He should be **honest**.

Naina: Hands down. Greed and dishonesty are just disgusting.

3) Vandana: **Non-violent personality**.

Naina: Hmm. No! Are you crazy? He should be able to defend his woman if the need arises. Not that I'd need defending, but...

Vandana: Non-violent, but he should not feel that he has to prove he is macho by beating up every little pest that annoys him. He should have a tight leash on his temper.

Naina: Hmm...too much testosterone like bulging muscles is just gross.

4) Vandana: Should be **family-loving**.

Naina: If he doesn't treat my brothers and sisters right, he is out of my life. I don't mind what he feels about my Mom and Dad, though.

Vandana: Naina they are your parents!

Naina: Whatever. Let us move forward.

5) Naina: He should be **gallant** and **chivalrous**.

Vandana: Yes, even though I am a real feminist by nature, it is good when the guy holds out the door for me.

Naina: Every guy holds out the door for you. We are talking about *my* Mr Right.

Vandana: You glare at every guy as though if he were walk

in front of you and open the door, you'll shoot him there and then.

Naina: Of course, I don't. You are being absurd.

Vandana: Yeah? Remember Mukul?

Naina: No.

Vandana: Of course, you don't. He has been in Prayag Hospital for the past three months after you…

Naina: Next.

Vandana: Ha! You…

6) Naina: Next. He **shouldn't be hard on the eyes** either.

Vandana: Oh, how could I forget such an important point? We'd have to move this to the second number, Naina.

Naina: Superficial missy.

Vandana: As if you aren't.

7) Vandana: He should be **compassionate**, **generous** and **kind.**

Naina: You know what is the problem with men who are kind, sensitive, generous and compassionate?

Vandana: What?

Naina: They already have boyfriends.

Vandana: I am serious, Naina. And I saw that joke in yesterday's *Delhi Times*.

Naina: I am serious, too. Life isn't a Georgette Heyer novel, Vandana.

Vandana: How do you know about Georgette Heyer novels? So I was right. I knew you read them too!

8) Naina: Oh, I almost forgot one. My last criterion is that he **shouldn't be financially dependent** on me.

Vandana: I totally agree. Cheapness is a big turn-off.

I put aside my pen and paper to wind up, "That's it."

Vandana snatches it back, "Nope."

9) Vandana: You forgot confidence. He should be **confident** but not over-confident.

Naina: Well, a man who always takes charge is sometimes sexy.

Vandana: Only you would think that, but alright, it is *your* list.

We gaze thoughtfully at the list.

I frown. "I am more romantic than I like to believe."

"You say that as if it is a bad thing."

"Isn't it?"

Vandana doesn't reply and turns thoughtful again. A small smile hovers on her lips.

"What?" I ask.

"Do you know who this list reminds me of?"

"Who?"

She closes her eyes, "This guy with whom I have a date tonight."

"You didn't tell me."

"I was getting there. We first met in school."

"Wow," I say. "Cute."

"No, I meant in the school in which I am teaching. He was accompanying one of my kindergarteners."

My mouth drops open, "Vandana! He is married? You won't…"

"He is Khushi's unmarried neighbour who has returned from New York after four years."

"Loaded?" I ask curiously.

She nods, "Filthy rich. He is what God had in mind when he created Adonis. And Khushi, the upper kindergarten's very own Hitler, dotes on him. She pulls up her skirt to show him the colour of her knickers at every opportunity she gets."

I cover my mouth with my hand, "Oh God, no. Tell me about it."

She shakes her head in sympathy, "Some girls don't understand how to play hard to get. But this guy, Aditya, is so sweet about it, he never minds it. He drops her to school daily because his neighbour is in her last month of pregnancy and the husband is busy in the office. So he qualifies seven of your nine qualities, leaving his honesty and chivalry in question. That I may get to know by midnight."

I grin as Vandana winks, "Well, good luck with your date. But what about me?"

"Haven't you understood by now? You're going man hunting."

"Thank you so much for eleborating."

I can sense her bristle with impatience, "See, this is what we are going to do. We are going to look for men that qualify that list. Then you will to go out on a date with them. After the man hunting is over, we'd have found our winner."

"My God, Vandana," I sit up, amazed, "you should be a military general."

She blushes prettily.

"So, who is my first date?"

She lapses into silence for a minute or two before moving towards the phone. While talking to her mother in Patiala, she takes down notes on a notepad.

I watch in amazement as she asks carefully phrased questions about everything, ranging from his sexuality to his favourite X-rated websites. After 15 minutes, she puts down the phone and says, "Meet my cousin Ritesh. He is our Victim #1."

Shriya Garg

Naina Kashyap's Potential Suitor, And Drumroll... Victim #1

By Vandana Sinha

Name: Ritesh Garg

Age: 29

Occupation: Marketing

Place of Ambush: Travertino, Oberoi.

Uniform: Vandana's black strapless cocktail dress with Vandana's black stilettos, a silver bracelet and matching ear-studs.

Height: 5'8".

Weight: 84 kg.

Physical Appearance: Tall, dark, white-capped teeth (as noticed by Vandana on their last meeting), brown hair and large hands.

Attractive Features: Is generous with his dates and loves food and cooking. Also has a very large family and is active with a local NGO.

Unattractive Feature(s): Calls his date names related to food, like 'Cherry Pie', 'Sugar Bread' and 'My Pink Strawberry'. Moreover, he is still hung up on his last girlfriend.

Interests: Food, cooking and expensive wine.

Atmosphere: Dim lighting and intimate conversation.

Beware: Avoid discussing his ex-girlfriend or past relationships.

His Ideal Woman: A headstrong person who is not afraid of speaking her mind; should share his interests and support him in his work for the poor; willing to overlook his stubbornness and sheer pigheadedness.

"I don't understand the point of writing all this," I complain, flexing my throbbing wrist.

"It is for your later dates, like if you're confused whether you've worn a particular dress before or not. This also organises things for later evaluation."

"Um," I nod and glance at the clock. With the enquiry and the lists and Vandana's telephone conversation with her cousin about his interests, it is evening already.

"Hey, Vandana, where are *you* going with this guy tonight?"

"I don't know. I told Aditya to take me any place he is comfortable."

"When is he picking you up?"

"Eight." She glances at the clock and hops up, "Oh, it is six already. I didn't notice how time flew. I need to start getting ready. What about you?"

I look moodily at the clothes and accessories she has laid out for me. "I have to get ready, too. I'll return your clothes tomorrow." I pick them up carefully and put them in my car.

"Wish me luck."

She hugs me instead. "I hope he is your Mr Right. Now, just remember not to talk too much. You don't want to scare him away on the first date. And he is taking you to Travertino, so behave."

"I am not an unruly pet of yours," I scowl. "Best of luck to you, too." and before she can reply, I dash off.

An hour later, as I come out of my room properly coiffured and dressed, Manya stops in her tracks, "Are you going to the circus?"

I open my mouth in outrage but close it. "Of course not," I finally say, checking my reflection in the glass cabinet of the dining room, "I am going man hunting."

"*Excuse me?*"

Shriya Garg

"Remember my six-month deal with Dad? I can hardly think of finding my future husband sitting at home, sulking about it."

"Vandana has fixed you up with someone, hasn't she?" Manya laughs.

"Am I that transparent?" I ask.

"Nope," she puts an arm around my shoulders. "You are just that obvious. Who is the poor guy?"

"A Ritesh Garg."

"Erm, nice name," she says but her tone implies otherwise.

"It is not bad; just a typical Indian name. Plus, Gargs are said to be real smart people."

"That remains to be seen. You told uncle?" she asks, referring to my father.

"I am not talking to him. Mom will tell him."

"You know he doesn't like you staying out so late."

"What else am I supposed to do? As if I like the prospect of sitting with a stranger in an expensive restaurant when I can stay at home, read a good book and spill Appy on my shorts."

"You are right. But you're looking really pretty."

Shaurya just then exits from his room. Since it is a Sunday, he is at home relaxing. On seeing me, he bursts out laughing. "Has hell officially frozen over?" Shaurya asks, gasping because he is laughing so hard.

"And take some pepper spray, just in case," Manya adds, ignoring him.

"Are you going out?" Shaurya asks as we move to the main door, waiting for my date to arrive.

"Yep."

Aunt Nandini rushes over, carrying a silver tray with a coconut, some red *roli* (vermillion powder) and a sweetmeat.

"God, can't I even go out in peace?"

"Here, eat this," she says, ignoring my protest and forces the *barfi* (sweetmeat) into my mouth and rotates the incense in my face. "God willing, you will find your husband in him."

"I hope so, too."

My phone rings. And I know Ritesh Garg has arrived.

"Ooh, Mercedes," Shaurya whistles, peeping from behind the drapery.

I wave them all goodbye and rush outside. Once near the door, I walk at a more sedate pace, trying to appear serene.

His teeth are really painted, is the first think I think as he smiles at me and holds out the door.

Chivalrous: Check.

"My! Vandana never told me that you are so beautiful," he says as his opening statement. And even though the line sounds rehearsed, I give the guy points for trying.

Gallant: Check.

Then he smiles again and thoughts of teeth-paint cloud my mind. I curb my irrational urge to confirm it from him. I know quite many people who could benefit from that. And no, Grandmom, I am not talking about you.

But despite that, he is quite handsome. He is not too tall, so he doesn't tower over me and he is not bald, has no moustache, is clean-shaven, well-dressed, doesn't wear gel in his hair and is not fat.

Handsome: Check.

The car journey passes quietly. Soft jazz music fills the leather interior. We make pleasant conversation and get to know each other because he doesn't know that I have his bio-data in my purse.

I tell him about my family, how the discussion of marriage arose, my views about arranged marriages and my man-hunting mission. I remember Vandana's warning regarding behaviour and try to act demure and polite.

He is quite surprised at my reaction towards Dad's suggestion and actually laughs over the eligibility list we've made.

"What happened that made you so averse to the idea of arranged marriages?" he asks. "As far as I know, love marriages are still an uncommon practice in middle-class families."

I don't like the way he uses the word 'middle-class families', but I let it go. "They are, but this is the 21st century. The idea of two people vowing to spend the rest of their lives together without even knowing each other properly is as absurd as all women wearing *burqa* in public. May be it is the culture of some religious or ethnic communities. But culture and custom are followed because they are appreciated and repeated. Why follow them just for the heck of it? Our aim in life is not to entangle ourselves in matrimony and increase the already high population of our country. Marriage is an important step – perhaps the most important – of our life and it does bear thinking." He is listening intently, so I continue because I am really passionate about this subject. "If you want to get married, do, but what is the point of accepting your family's choice? They are not going to live with that person for the rest of their lives. We are intelligent adults and know more than our parents of what we want in our spouse. We call the West advanced and modern, as if it is a bad thing. Have you ever heard that half of *their* marriages are arranged?"

Ritesh stops the car and the valet steps forward for the keys. He helps me out and replies, "If what you are saying is right, then why do they have a higher divorce rate than ours? Almost 50 per cent."

"That is only a matter of opinion. In India's middle-class society, a divorcee is a social pariah. People think a thousand times before divorcing – which should be done – and in the end, decide not to take the step because of the children or parents or society. It is your life. Why let others dictate your actions?"

Ritesh smiles. "I see that you aren't afraid to speak your mind. I like that in a woman."

I almost say, "I know," but stop myself in time and smile politely instead.

The waiter shows us our seats but before we can re-continue our debate, his cell phone rings.

Okay, one thing you should know about me: I really hate it when people take out their cell phones and ignore the people around them. I have known some people who keep texting other friends even when somebody is talking to them. It really is annoying. But, of course, Ritesh has got a call from an important business associate which he cannot ignore. So he excuses himself and leaves the table without even ordering anything.

I pretend to read my menu card as the waiter hovers near my elbow, hoping he will be back soon but there is no sign of him even after 10 minutes.

Just then I hear someone call out, "Naina!" I automatically duck my head because nothing is more embarrassing than being caught dining alone in an expensive restaurant. However, it turns out that I shouldn't have bothered because the voice belatedly registers in my ears as Vandana's.

"Vandana! What are you doing here?" I ask and then notice the handsome God standing next to her – Aditya Khanna.

Vandana beams at me, "Aditya decided to bring me here at Travertino's. What an amazing coincidence, isn't it?"

"Yeah," I say. Aditya Khanna is a typical fairy-tale prince – tall, dark and handsome, with unpainted white teeth that are smiling politely at me as he waits for an introduction.

"Aditya, this is Naina, my best friend," Vandana introduces us. His brows raise a little, like every man's does when a woman like me is introduced as little Vandana's best friend, but he holds out his hand and smiles charmingly.

"Where is Ritesh?" she asks, looking around for my date.

"An important business associate called," I say and am gratified to see Vandana properly annoyed.

"Really, this is no way to treat a lady." Her face acquires a mulish expression that I know very well, but Aditya apparently doesn't, because his eyes widen on seeing the change in the personality of his polite, sweet date. She sees Ritesh approaching and takes off, probably to give him a piece of her mind. Aditya's eyes follow her, but the pressure of my hand on his arm shatters his fantasy which leaves my way clear.

"Look, I know guys like you very well," I lie, giving him my best menacing look. "If you ever, *ever* even *think* of hurting her, think once more."

His eyebrows shoot up. Impressed by my own performance, I straighten my shoulders and pull myself up to my impressive 5'8".

"You break her heart and I'll break your face," I add.

His brows rise so high that they are barely visible beneath the lock of hair dangling over his forehead. I have just begun enjoying my role as Mother Hen when Vandana and Ritesh return.

Maybe it is my smug smile or Aditya's slightly dazed expression that alerts her, but Vandana's eyes narrow in suspicion. I give her my best innocent smile.

"Do you want to double?" Ritesh asks once the two men have been introduced.

"No!" Aditya and I say together. "I mean," I quickly amend, "some other time. For the time being I just want to get to know you. It is our first date, after all." I smile at him.

Ritesh flushes and smiles back. Vandana takes one look at his teeth and grins at me. I know that both of us are thinking the same thing.

Painted teeth: Yeah, check.

Just before both of them turn away to their respective tables, I pat my purse pointedly and whisper to Aditya, "I have pepper spray in here."

I overhear Vandana telling him not to pay me any attention because I am just an accountant and not a cop. Aditya laughs heartily because he thinks she is joking. If only she was!

"I am so sorry for the phone call, sweetie pie," Ritesh says and I mentally groan.

We order some white wine and hors d'oeuvres, dismiss the waiter and continue the conversation from where we'd left off.

"Do you like cooking?" he asks.

My fork drops to the ground. In an effort to buy myself some time, so as to think of a suitable reply, I bend under the table to retrieve it.

"Do I like to cook?" I mutter to myself. "Why would any sane woman want to?"

Suddenly, my thoughts scatter and I freeze. My eyes are at level with his below the belt area and his zip is open.

I bite my lip to hide my laughter and then it dies as soon as it has come. Peeking from the little empty space between the two sides of the zipper is something brownish in colour.

Omigosh!

"Naina, are you okay?" he asks from far away – probably still above the table.

I straighten immediately and bump my head against the metal. "Yes, yes," I babble as clammy sweat breaks out on my forehead. "Why won't I be?"

But my mind is still down below and I am unable to concentrate on anything except the colour brown. The scene keeps flashing in my mind and the more I try not to think about it, the more it persists.

"So, as I was saying, I just love Italian food. There is

Shriya Garg

something about it…Naina, honey, are you sure, you're okay? You seem a little pale? Don't you like Italian food?"

"I do, I do. Of course, I do," I stammer. "Pizza is absolutely my favourite," I laugh nervously because something about liking pizza strikes me as hilarious. At the same time, a part of my brain is chanting, brown. Skin, black.

Ew. I grimace.

"Naina?" he asks again, concerned as he sees me grimace. "Doesn't your food taste good?"

"No, no, I believe…please, excuse me," I mutter and flee towards the rest room.

Once there, I stare at my over-bright eyes and flushed skin in the mirror and stifle a giggle. I fix my make-up, giggle, take a few deep breaths, giggle, go back and giggle again.

"I do believe, Ritesh, that you're right. I am feeling much better now," I lie.

The main course arrives and we chatter about our respective families and jobs. The evening is proceeding very well when I just cannot resist, and drop my spoon again. Sue me.

"Oops," I say and bend.

I am just confirming, not peeking! I am making sure that the open zip isn't just a result of my overactive imagination.

Two seconds later I have my answer.

It is not.

"So, Ritesh, tell me," I say hastily, in an effort to drag my mind from the gutter. "Have you been in any serious relationship?"

Too late, I remember Vandana's word of caution.

He puts down his fork, his eyes cloud and the smile vanishes. I touch his hand briefly but he is too far gone to notice it.

"Naina, I do believe you are right. We have skirted the topic long enough. We both know why we are sitting here. We are looking for our respective soulmate and thinking of finding it in each other. But I want to tell you something," he continues in a faraway voice and I stare at him moodily. I do not find guys carrying a torch for another girl romantic. It is actually pathetic. If he wants a girl, he should get her, and if he can't, then get on with his life. The past in no place to look to if you want a good future.

So he is telling me the tragic story of his young puppy love with an angel called Aishwarya and my mind begins wandering again to the same old thing – his zip.

He begins eating again and I get a strange feeling that he is about to weep.

Please don't cry. Please, please don't cry. I want a sensitive man for myself but not *that* sensitive.

He does not notice the way I am tapping my spoon against my palm in boredom and I can't help myself any more. I give in to the temptation, "Ritesh, why aren't you wearing any underwear?"

I just want to distract him. It's a noble thing to do, if you really think about it.

As soon as the words are out of my mouth, I realise what I have said.

There is complete silence from the opposite side of the table. I slowly open my eyes, millimetre by millimetre and notice that he has frozen with his fork held midway to his mouth. His eyes are as wide as saucers and he looks at me with an expression which says that he is choking on his food.

"I am sorry!" I explain in a rushed tone. "It was an accident, I promise. My fork dropped and your zip was open and something was flashing and I thought that…"

I break off when he starts coughing. I hand him water but he pushes it away. His coughing turns more violent. He falls out of his chair on to the floor and a waiter, who had been going

Shriya Garg

past us just at that moment carrying two trays of food, trips over his body and spills food all over Ritesh.

But what worries me is that he still hasn't stopped coughing. His back almost arches off the floor. People have started gathering around us and I freak out when I realise that he isn't coughing. He is *choking* on his food.

I wring my hands helplessly, my mind frozen with shock. The restaurant staff is busy arranging for an ambulance and shouting whether there is a doctor anywhere among the guests.

Aditya and Vandana rush out of the crowd that is staring at Ritesh as if he is some alien species. Come to think of it, he kind of looks like one because of all the pasta and gravy covering his expensive suit and because of the odd noises he is making.

"Let me, let me," Aditya shouts, making his way towards Ritesh. "I have some training in first-aid." He screams at me, "Naina, what was he eating?"

I am too shocked to get the import of his question. I ask "Huh?"

"What was he eating before he choked? Everybody, please clear the way. Give him space to breathe!"

"Sweetie," Vandana says to me gently but urgently, "what was he eating when he choked?"

I am finally about to answer when Ritesh says something and Aditya bends down on his knees to hear him better, "Yes, Ritesh? What are you saying?"

"Sk..Sk…" he gasps and everybody strains to hear what he has to stay. "Ski…" he tries again and his back almost arches off the floor again with the effort. "Skin…under, under…"

"Yes," Aditya cajoles, pressing his ear next to his mouth. "Skin under what?"

But I already know what he is trying to say and I cover my face with my hands. I want to scream. I have heard that people can die of choking and here Ritesh is clarifying his *clothing*.

"Sk…skin coloured underwear."

Silence greets Ritesh's little speech.

And then Vandana wails, "Naina, what have you done *this* time?"

I am saved from answering as the restaurant manager and the maitre d' prepare to load him on to a stretcher and take him away. The ambulance has arrived.

"Oh my God," Vandana sobs.

Do you know how people laugh on reading a novel where the protagonist uses the phrase, "*I could just die of mortification*?"

Well, let me tell you then that it is *not* funny when it is used in your own context.

Even though it has been scientifically proved that people *cannot* die of embarrassment and because I do not wish to be the only exception to the rule, I take out my phone from my borrowed tote bag, and hit #1 on the speed dial.

"I think I might have killed my date," I answer when the phone is picked up.

* * * * *

An hour later, we all are in the hospital, waiting for Ritesh's report, when Shaurya arrives, first looking concerned, then angry at me for going out with such a person and finally, when I explain to him the story, he clutches his sides with laughter. My brother really has a warped sense of humour.

Vandana doesn't want to smile but even the corners of her lips begin to twitch, much against her wishes. Aditya, the only person who doesn't know the entire story, keeps glaring at the whole lot of us.

When Shaurya finally notices how upset I am, he puts an arm around me but continues to laugh. "Shaurya Kashyap, Naina's lawyer," he says to Aditya. If Aditya thinks it weird that

Shriya Garg

I am hugging my lawyer, he doesn't comment but extends his palm to shake hands.

"Do you really think he is going to sue me?" I ask Shaurya, glancing at him from the corner of my eyes.

"There is a distinct possibility. Let us just hope he gets alright first."

It turns out that he is alright. I mean there is nothing serious about his condition – just mild abrasions in his throat because of the bone he'd choked on. He'd live.

I go in and see him. He can barely speak but assures me that he isn't angry with me and instead finds the whole situation very funny.

Sense of humour: Check.

I am glad and tell him so. We exchange numbers and promise to meet again sometime next week. I thank Aditya for all his help despite knowing the fact that he stayed because Ritesh was Vandana's cousin, though I knew I'd spoiled their date. So I take him aside and grudgingly apologise.

"What is the use now?" he asks.

"Hey, I am trying to be nice here, you jerk."

"You? Nice? God's very own Satan? No, thank you very much."

My mouth falls open, "You annoying idiot. I don't understand what Vandana sees in you."

His eyes narrow and he straightens, towering menacingly over me, "You should be glad that I don't call girls names. "But, I can't see what Vandana sees in you either!" he finishes with a triumphant smile. "There, and I didn't call you any name either."

"At least I am not a pretentious jerk," I say, pointing to his expensive suit and polished shoes.

"But definitely an irritating witch."

"Watch your tongue!" I warn.

"Hello, pot, don't call the kettle black. Who asks a man about his underwear on the first date?" the tenor of his voice rises. Thank God, Vandana is still inside with Ritesh.

I smirk, "Oh yeah, like you weren't thinking about *your* date's underwear!" I refuse to drag Vandana into it and thus, cleverly use the phrase 'your date'.

"My date isn't a man!"

I pretend surprise, "Oh, and you are?"

This is such a lie. I haven't seen this much testosterone filled in a suit since…well, I've never seen it.

He scowls and I know I have crossed the line by doubting his manliness.

"I have never felt like raising a hand on a woman but you certainly tempt me!"

"Aditya!" Vandana gasps and I barely manage to control my smile. *Deal with that, Spiderman.*

"What is going on here, you two?" she asks angrily.

"Ask your irritating best friend."

"Ask your jerk of a boyfriend," I counter derisively.

"Stop creating a scene, you two," Shaurya intervenes, placing an arm between us.

"Not my fault," I sniff. "It is all because of this unformed foetus that got ejected long before its time had come."

Aditya doesn't miss a beat; I give him full credit for that. "People who live in glass houses shouldn't throw stones at others. Hasn't anybody taught you that, you beautiful piece of decomposed vegetable matter?"

I gasp, "I am sure that way deep, deep, deep, deep, way deep down, you're a good…no, scratch that, an *okay* person." And because my sentence feels incomplete to me, I add smugly, "Dogpiss."

His eyes narrow, "Oh, shut up, you human virus...oh, Vandana!"

Both of us stop when somebody sobs next to us. Vandana is crying softly, her big eyes accusing.

"Vandana, I am so sorry!" I say and immediately hug her, glowering at Aditya because it is entirely his fault. He refuses to rise to the bait.

"I didn't mean to upset you, Vandana," his tone completely changes.

"I know," she says, taking the handkerchief he has offered. "But it has been such a horrible evening. What with Ritesh's accident and then you two fighting."

"I know, I know, sweetheart," I console her. "I am so sorry for spoiling your evening."

"Oh no, it is not your fault, Naina."

We manage to stop her tears within the next five minutes. Shaurya gives me an impatient look. He is waiting for me to mop this mess up. I have thought more than once that he has a soft spot for Vandana and I even tease him about it. So when he pretends that he doesn't care seeing Vandana cry like this, I do not smile.

She is a year older than him. It would be a scandal and despite what people seem to believe, I do not create a scandal wherever I go. So, as soon as Ritesh's family arrives and Vandana stops crying, I quietly follow Shaurya out of the hospital.

Aditya Khanna is really pissed off at Naina Kashyap. In the one week since their first disastrous meeting, she had made his love-life hell. It seems that whenever he goes to Vandana's house, she is there. And if he and Vandana want to go out, she is there too.

Just thinking about their last encounter makes him wince. They'd fought in Vandana's garden like 11-year olds. He'd pulled her hair and she'd actually *kicked* him. His favourite pair of jeans were now lying in the back of the cupboard, torn from where her heels had made contact with his leg.

He is sitting brooding on the sofa in his apartment, when his phone rings.

"Hey, man," one of his colleagues from New York asks, "How are you?"

"Hi, Nitin. I am alright. You?"

"Pretty much the same. How is India?"

"Amazing," Aditya answers truthfully. "I hadn't realised how much I'd missed it until I came back."

"That is a good thing."

"Why?" Aditya asks warily.

"I am coming to India, buddy. My parents want me to get married to an Indian girl."

"Ouch."

"Tell me about it."

"So when are you landing?"

"Tomorrow."

"That soon?"

"Yeah, man, my parents have got me excited about marriage and my *suhag-raat*." At the mention of his wedding night with a sweet little Indian virgin, he chucks lecherously. "By any chance, do you know any nice Indian girl looking for a groom?"

Shriya Garg

Aditya is about to say, no, when he suddenly thinks of Naina. An idea begins taking shape in his mind. She had destroyed his first date and now it was his turn to score a point.

"I have one in my mind"

Naina Kashyap's Potential Suitor, Victim #2

By Vandana Sinha

Name: Nitin Sean.

Age: 32.

Occupation: CEO of a branch of Adobe in New York.

Place of Ambush: Café Coffee Day, Connaught Place.

Height: 5'9".

Weight: 78 kg.

Physical Appearance: Medium height, blue eyes, tanned face and blond hair.

Uniform: Yellow, knee-length frock with Vandana's yellow pumps.

Attractive Features: Very astute and clever; naïve about women. Strange for a New Yorker because he has been very homely till college; sweet and selfless.

Unattractive Feature(s): A little clumsy and has armpit hair which he proudly shows off; is Aditya's colleague; stammers when he is nervous.

Interests: Singing, marriage and women.

Atmosphere: Lively ambience with bright, joyful conversation.

Beware: Don't ask him to sing.

His Ideal Woman: A woman who can combine Indian wisdom and culture with the Western sciences.

"I am not sure I like the sound of him," I tell Vandana as we sit in my room to review her handiwork.

"At least meet him once," she replies with an exasperated look. "It isn't like you have any other option."

She is right. Since I have refused another date with Ritesh after the choking incident because I fear for his life, I am running out of potential grooms.

"But look at the armpit-hair thing," I point out, tapping the paper with my index finger. "It is *gross*."

"Aditya says that Nitin may be a little weird but he is very nice," Vandana recites loyally.

I give her one of my 'I-told-you-that-Aditya-is-crazy, didn't-I' looks. "All the more reason to distrust Nitin."

Vandana has stopped taking my comments to heart. Earlier, she used to get very upset whenever I put that boyfriend of hers down, but lately she seems more amused.

Ria barges into my room just then. It is late at night and she must have finished her homework. "Are you guys talking about Aditya again?" she asks, peering down at the sheet in my hand, over my shoulder.

We nod. They've met once when he had come to pick Vandana up and she was at my home. Ria had fallen in love with him then.

The reason behind this is obvious. Ria claims that the love of her life is Shahid Kapoor. She is crazy about him. She has all his films on CDs, has hung his posters in her room and was on cloud nine when Shahid's movie *Jab We Met* was released because he plays the character whose name is Aditya Kashyap.

"I won't have to change my name after marriage now," she had wept happily as she read the newspaper in front of her.

When I pointed out that same surnames meant that they could be related and Aditya Kashyap could be a long-distance cousin, she had stamped her foot and left the room.

So when she found out that Vandana's boyfriend went by the name Aditya, she'd already passed the verdict without even seeing his face. The fact that he looked like Adonis had certainly helped.

"Aw, Vandana, you are so lucky," Ria gives a silly grin and I glare at her to leave the room.

"Hey," she says, glaring right back, "at least *she* knows how to keep a man."

I aim a pillow at her but she dodges it. I ask, "Correct me if I am wrong, but when did I ask you for your opinion?"

She ignores me and snatches the sheet out of my hand. Taking a bite out of an apple, she studies it with interest, "Let us see what you have here. Holy cow! Armpit hair!"

"Exactly," I say triumphantly to Vandana, glad to have someone on my side.

"But he is Aditya's friend," Vandana complains.

Ria's ears twitch and she looks up. "Then he's got to be nice," she announces and puts the sheet away.

"Exactly like I said," Vandana smiles.

"You traitors," I say and give them a contemptuous look..

Ria dismisses the insult with a wave of her hands. "I hope you don't land him in a hospital."

My shoulders slump and I look at the sheet again. "I hope so too," I finally say with a deep sigh.

"Hi, I am Nitin Sean," says Nitin, getting up as soon as I see him in the little loveseat at Café Coffee Day.

Chivalrous: Check.

I shake his hand and smile. "Naina Kashyap," I introduce myself.

Though I am prepared for the armpit part, it is a shock to see those yellowish-brown things glistening proudly like dew-laden leaves in the morning. But I console myself with the fact that at least his teeth aren't painted.

We order some coffee and he comments on my yellow dress. "Your dress is brighter and hotter than the Indian sun," he says.

I smile absently.

Gallant: Check.

"So, what are you doing in India?" I make small talk.

"Looking for a bride. My parents want to see me settled and bouncing children on my lap."

"Indian parents?"

"Father," he sighs. There is this American accent in his voice which is really cute. I smile back a little and add, "That explains it."

"I am sorry, but I didn't get what you meant."

I tell him my story and add, "They can't wait to see henna on my hands."

"Henna?" he asks. I tell him about the green mixture with which we paint our hands and he smiles. "Oh, yeah, I remember. It looks really pretty."

"Yeah, but it is really messy."

He nods. A couple of seconds later, he adds, "I have never

been to India before but whatever I've seen in a day fascinates me. New Delhi equals New York in terms of diversity."

"So they say."

"But the poverty here is unimaginable."

You've seen nothing, boy.

I nod reluctantly, "India has some of nature's most astounding visions and some of the world's most appalling poverty."

His brows draw together in a frown, "Yes, but let us not talk about that. Tell me about your job. You're an accountant, aren't you?"

"Yes."

"But you don't look like an accountant."

I laugh and there is genuine amusement in it, "People are always surprised when I tell them that. I still haven't figured out the reason."

"It is because of the way you look," he begins in a know-it-all voice.

I give him a flirtatious smile, "How do I look?"

"Oh, you know," he waves a hand towards the dress which Vandana took an hour to put together. "No offence, but you're a babe. Accountants, however, are typically short and skinny. They wear tweed jackets or starched shirts and skirts. Plus, the spectacles are missing. Not this sexy little outfit."

I don't like the way his gaze keeps sliding down the neck of the dress every couple of seconds but I curb it. "I am flattered," I say. Maybe I should go to the theatre, I think, since I lie so well.

"Come on, don't tell me you don't hear this a hundred times a day."

I chuckle, "Now I am *really* flattered."

He laughs at my comment and we chatter some more. He

tells me about his job and family as we finish the cake and order some more coffee.

I am almost sure that this is going to turn out to be a good afternoon when the guy hired to play the guitar gets up for a break.

"You are really pretty, Naina," Nitin says, looking directly into my eyes. "I want to sing something that is worthy of your beauty."

"Uh," I glance at the guitar propped up against the empty elevated platform. "No, it is okay, Nitin."

"No, it is not." He gets up and eyes the guitar and mike, "Tell me, do you like Bryan Adams?"

I sink lower into my seat, "Not much…"

"Watch me," he replies with a confident smile. "I am going to change your opinion."

And before I can protest, he walks up to the stage with long, purposeful strides. "Ladies and gentlemen," he says into the mike and conversation breaks off all around us. That is when I notice someone on the table next to me – Aditya.

He waves to me, winks and turns towards Nitin with a smirk on his face.

"I want to sing something for a very special person whom I hope I would have the pleasure of knowing some more. But for now, Naina, this is for you."

The girls sitting around me look at me with a wistful expression. "Aw, this guy is so cute," I hear one of them whisper.

My uneasiness vanishes a little. How bad could he sing? I think and shrug. I smile back at him and watch as he takes a sip of water and clears his throat. Very professional.

"*Look into my eyes,*" Nitin finally begins in an *awful* voice. "*You will see…*"

Just seven words. That's all. And I Know he is worse than me.

And *that* is definitely saying something because every time I sing, Shaurya swears to God that all dogs in the 10-mile radius would come out of their homes and begin howling.

"It is because they hear their friend sing and want to join her," Shaurya would say with a perfectly innocent expression on his face – an expression which I have seen him master in front of the mirror. Seriously.

"*Search your heart, search your soul...*" Nitin arches his throat to look up at the ceiling, closes his eyes, clutches the mike tighter and bellows. Immediately, the wistful expressions in the faces of the girls vanish. I see through their eyes how he arches his back and rotates his hips completely out of rhythm and makes smacking sounds with his lips every time he opens them to sing.

They raise their eyebrows at each other and then shoot me discreet looks. Only Aditya looks happy as he encourages Nitin. "Yeah, buddy, you're awesome," Aditya hoots and the others look at him as though he is crazy.

"*You know it is true...Everything I do, I do it for you...*" Nitin tilts the mike and bends on his knees, like they do on TV – I am not even kidding, I wish I was – and continues howling like a wolf, complete with shaking of his head from side to side as though he is high on something. When he draws to the end – finally – he opens his eyes and smiles gratefully at Aditya. Aditya winks back.

Worse than his singing are his actions. He plays the air-guitar with his fly. How old is he? *Sixteen?* And the way he is moving his waist...in complete eights which look more like horribly-twisted vertical ones. His voice cracks, but he is so happy that he doesn't notice. "*There is no love...like your love, and no other, could give me more love.*"

"Please, someone make him shut up," somebody whispers not too silently in another corner.

"Who is he singing for?"

"Poor woman."

Great God, please bless Bryan Adams for making the song this short, I think, as he sings, "*You know its true, everything I do...ahh...I do it for you.*"

Aditya and I are the only people who applaud.

Please don't say my name. Please don't say my name. Please don't...

"This is for the beautiful lady sitting in yellow over there." And as if that is not enough, he points towards me and *bows*. "Naina Kashyap, I hope we have many more memorable moments like this."

My '*stop shitting, shithead*' hangs unsaid in the air. "Uh..." I stammer.

Despite the obvious disinterest among his audience, his smile doesn't waver and he never breaks the eye contact. You got to admire the man for his self-confidence. He blinks once with an incredibly tender look in his eyes. My anger evaporates there and then.

There is something really lovable about a man embarrassing himself to impress a woman. So when the people look at me with varying degrees of horror, I smile at him, "Sure."

Aditya stops smiling.

Nitin thanks Aditya as well, and straightening himself, makes his way towards me. With a broad grin on his face, he stops opposite me and pulls out his chair. And in his excitement, pulls it too much. My warning comes too late.

He misjudges the distance and sits down on empty air.

"Oomph!" he falls down on all fours. Aditya looks up at the ceiling with a knowing look and smacks his forehead in a gesture that screams, *of course, with Naina Kashyap, it just* had *to happen.*

Nitin laughs awkwardly at his clumsiness and ignoring my

outstretched hand, places a hand on the table and pulls himself up.

"Are you okay?" I ask.

"Yes, yes, absolutely. Do remain seated."

I nod uncertainly and finally say, "That was a nice song."

He stops checking out his scratched hand and looks up at me with twinkling eyes, "When Aditya said that you'd love it if I sang a song for you, I didn't believe him. But now I see he was right." He takes my hand in his and turns towards Aditya, "Thanks, mate."

I angrily snatch my hand away from Nitin's. "Excuse me," I say to him and march towards Aditya's table.

I motion toward the door, and grinning at Nitin, he makes a show of yawning and stretching out all his limbs before following me...the *pig!* "You are such an insensitive jackass," I say as soon as we are out of eyesight and earshot.

He folds his arms and leans against the wall. Casually inspecting his fingernails, he says, "That is just your embarrassment talking."

"I can't believe you let your friend be humiliated like that! I am so glad that I am not your friend," I punctuate each word with a poke at his chest. "If you behave this way to your loved ones, I wonder what you'd do to your enemies. But...oh Lord," I pretend to exclaim, "I actually have a first-hand knowledge of what you do to your enemies."

My poking at his chest stops his smile. Warm colour rushes to his cheeks and his hands clench into fists on either side.

Einstein that I am, I do not take the hint. "What had the guy done to you?" I continue ranting. "Nothing! But *you* had to embarrass him like that in front of so many people just so that *you* could get your revenge. What a *petty,* small-minded man you are!"

Shriya Garg

"Hey!" Aditya replies indignantly. "What he doesn't know can't hurt him. He thinks that people actually like his singing. And when they leave the place wherever he sings, he thinks that they are just *jealous* of his talent."

"Oh yeah? Tell me another one."

In a motion that is too quick for such a large man, he unglues himself from the wall and takes a step towards me, "Are you calling me a liar?"

"No! I am calling you a liar *and* a jackass!"

"How dare you call me a jackass, you nerd?"

"Like this," I reply tartly. "*Jackass.*"

"You…you…" he thinks of something to say. "You *accountant!*"

I cannot help it. I gasp, "You say as if it is a bad thing."

He gives me a once-over, "With you, it is."

I know that we are creating a scene in the middle of the road, but I don't care. I am too furious to care. No one in my entire life of 25 years has ever riled me like this man.

In my defence, I have never been a violent person. I usually prefer to maim and kill with my tongue, rather than my hands. But he turns out to be the only person immune to my poison. I've been pushed too far. I retaliate by pushing him – literally, not figuratively – in return.

The next thing I know, he is lying face-first into a half-full garbage bin. It is one of those large bins that are put in big markets like CP which can accommodate at least six grownups.

As soon as the adrenalin fades, apprehension settles in my stomach. I glance nervously at him to judge his reaction, but he is too shocked to say anything. He just opens and closes his mouth. His eyes blink rapidly.

"Ugh," he finally says with as much as dignity as possible in such a circumstance and glances down at his clothes.

I dissolve into laughter as he emerges with his shirt splattered with different kinds of half-eaten foodstuffs and paper plates. There are some noodles poking out of his hair which manage to give him the air of a dirty mop. Despite all that, to my utmost disgust, he manages to look so adorable that I want to push him in all over again.

People around us start laughing.

He ignores them and instead turns his face up to the heavens. Scowling, he demands indignantly, "Why *me*? I am not even dating her!"

We both continue looking at the sky, but there is, of course, no reply. My stupidity would not make them break their silence.

He sighs and turns to look at me, "If you know what is good for you, you're going to run as fast as you can in the opposite direction."

I may be stupid but I am not suicidal, so I hastily follow his instructions to the letter.

"Nitin, I have to go. My lunch hour is about to get over," I say to my deranged date.

He nods, gets up and walks me to my car. He takes my keys and opens the door for me. Before climbing in, I turn and kiss him on the cheek. He actually blushes and keeps a hand on the door to steady himself. I am too happy from my encounter with Aditya and the date with him to notice it. I get in, wave and quickly slam the door shut.

"OUCH!"

Christ! In my haste and happiness, I fail to notice his fingers pressed tightly between the door and the frame.

I immediately throw open the door, "Oh gosh, I am so sorry!"

I didn't think it was possible to scream, yelp, cry, clutch

one's hand and jump at the same time, but Nitin somehow accomplishes it. His fingers are blue and swollen. I think I see blood.

Suddenly, Aditya appears from somewhere behind him. His green T-shirt still has stains of the garbage, but his hands are clean. He is trying very hard not to smile.

"What are you doing here?" I shout. While within myself I am thinking, *why him? Why* him?

"I had an intuition," he replies, not even trying to hide his smirk.

He takes Nitin's elbow, "Stop jumping around and let me take you to the hospital before any other bomb explodes over here."

* * * * *

"You pushed Aditya into a garbage bin *and* managed to put Nitin in the hospital — all in five minutes? Really, I've got to ask, Naina, how do you manage to do this?"

"This is not funny, Vandana," I say sourly.

It is about an hour after the accident that I am sitting in my cabin, using the office phone for my personal calls.

"So, how is Nitin now?" Vandana asks.

"I don't know. Aditya told me to take off for the office before I get both of them cremated. He said he'd convey Nitin's news."

She gives a wistful sigh, "He is so nice."

"Yeah," I answer without a pause, "like a stinking bulldog."

"Naina!"

"Sorry," I mutter.

"You shouldn't have pushed him into the garbage bin. I haven't seen you act so childish since Class VII," she scolds me and I moodily doodle on the notepad in front of me.

"I know I shouldn't have done that but there is something about that arrogant smirk of his which just brings out the worst in me. When I think of the names I called him I could just die of shame."

She laughs, "I think this has gone on long enough. You should really get on amiable terms with him."

"But he started it! He deliberately tried to embarrass me. Do you know Nitin can't sing to save his life? Do *you*?"

"Of course not," she says coolly. "But you paid him back, didn't you? Do you know how much of a cleanliness freak Aditya is? And he hates noodles. You're lucky he is too much of a gentleman to hit a girl."

I snort and then I sigh, "You're right, I guess. I did some really, unforgiveable things too."

Vandana senses victory, "You know, it is not too late to apologise."

I shoot out of my chair, "*Apologise?* Who said anything about *apologising?*"

"If you can put this immaturity behind you, apologising is the next obvious step."

I am speechless for a second. Then, "No!"

"Yes, sweetie. Here, this is his address," she recites it but I don't note it down. "When he calls you with Nitin's news, ask him when he can see you."

"But why can't I just apologise on the phone?"

"Naina…" I slowly sink back into my chair.

"Okay, fine. Give me the address."

That evening, I knock on his door.

"Who is it?" his voice asks from the other side.

"It is Naina."

The door is immediately wrenched open.

"What are *you* doing here?" he stands there – shirtless – with hair wet from a shower and water droplets still clinging to the fine hair sprinkled over his chest.

"Are you so poor that you cannot afford a new shirt?" I ask at the same time. But my gun has no ammunition in it, because I am still drooling over that Levi-clad body.

He must have noticed my gaze because the next thing he did was to cross his arms protectively across his chest.

I stare open-mouthed at the action, "Isn't this something a girl is supposed to do?"

"Not when the girl is the Taliban's leader."

I raise my brows and in a voice heavily laced with sarcasm, I say, "You're a laugh riot, Aditya."

"And yet, funnier than you," he replies and makes no move to invite me inside.

I grind my teeth and try to be nice, "May I come inside… please?"

"Are you choking on something?"

"No."

He strokes his chin, "You sure sound like that."

I grind my teeth again and pray for patience.

He finally sighs and turns to walk back inside. I leave the door open and follow him to his room.

Vandana was right: he *is* a cleanliness freak. Though the bold colours and scarce furniture scream his bachelorhood, the room is way too neat. There aren't even any dirty underclothes strewn around.

The house is big, airy and has an assortment of sleek Italian furniture and Indian patchwork.

"No way have you furnished this," I say as he grabs another green T-shirt, similar to the one I'd spoiled and gets into it.

"My sister," his voice is muffled due to the shirt.

"No parents?"

"In Greater Noida," he replies and turns to the mirror to comb his hair with his fingers.

I look around and spot a book lying upside down on the side-table. Before I can make out the name, his gaze follows mine and he immediately snatches it up.

"Hey," I say indignantly, trying to get hold of the book behind his waist but he stuffs it inside the cupboard.

"What?" I tease him. "Aditya Khanna reading a dirty novel?" I try to go past him and into the cupboard, but he catches hold of my wrists and doesn't let go.

"I tried once," he says dryly, "but no, nothing like that."

"Liar," I shake my head in disgust. "What else could be the problem?" I tug to get my hands free but after a not-too-brief glimpse of those muscles, I am not surprised at the steel grip. I tug harder still.

He sighs in exasperation, "You're not going to let it go, are you?"

"Nope, never."

He drops my wrists and takes out the book – *Harry Potter and the Order of Phoenix.*

His face wears a resigned look. "Go on, mock me. I can see you're just dying to comment on my IQ."

I am too shocked to do that. "You…how…Harry…but…"

"But just for your information," he continues in the same resigned tone, "I am an IIT and IIM-A graduate."

"You like *Harry Potter?*" Even to my ears my voice sounds shocked.

"Yeah, a Harry Potter nerd and proud of it," he says tonelessly and adds "not."

"My *whole* life I've been made fun of…I was *so* sure that no adult except me liked it."

His eyes widen dramatically, "*You* like Harry Potter? *You?* The very incarnation of Tom Marvolo Riddle?"

The strange feeling of kinship that had blossomed due to

our common interest in me deflates with a pop. I bristle with annoyance, "Shut up, muggle. Seriously, I never pegged you for a Harry Potter fan."

"Me neither, slytherin. And despite knowing that I am too old for it, I can't just escape it. I mean," he says with disgust, "seventh graders read it. And here I am."

I nod but do not really pay attention. "Favourite character?" I ask quickly.

"Severus Snape," he replies without a second's delay.

"What?" I am rightfully appalled. "Are you *insane*?"

A look comes into his eyes that I've seen only once before. That was 15 years ago when Mom told Ria that Santa Claus wasn't real.

His mouth sets into a firm line and he tilts his chin up, "Haven't you read *Deathly Hallows?* Nobody except Joanne Kathleen Rowling could have succeeded in creating such a multi-faceted character. The man has so many layers to him and unravelling each layer is like opening a long-buried treasure."

I immediately go on the defensive, "Ha! No way. Tom Marvolo Riddle a.k.a. Voldemort is the best character ever created. Have you ever seen his nose? It is adorable."

He blinks once, twice, thrice. "You," he says, shaking his head again, "are *crazy.*"

I ignore that statement. "Quick, favourite spell?"

"Sectumsempra."

"Hmm...there just might be hope for you after all. Gryffindor?"

"What else?"

We share a grin and I ask, "Harry and Hermione?"

"True love."

I chuckle and that is when it occurs to me that I am fraternising with the enemy.

I groan and hop up and down. "Quick," I say, closing my eyes tightly, "say something bad."

"What?"

I hop even quicker. "No, no, this cannot be happening," I mutter to myself. "We can't be becoming friends." Louder, I say, "Something bad, please, I beg of you!"

He obliges happily, "Okay, you cheap, drunken whore, what are you doing here?"

I choke, "*Excuse me*?"

"Oh, too much?"

"Yes."

He grins, "Let me try again." He even clears his throat and bows a little, "Madam Expensive, sober accountant, why have you decided to finally grace this lowly peasant with the pleasure of your company?"

"Much better," I nod regally. "I am here to apologise for pushing you in that bin."

"What?" Immediately straightening from his servile position, he cups a hand behind his ear and mocks me, "What are you saying? I can't hear anything."

"Sorry," I roll my eyes and repeat my apology.

"Strangest thing," he laughs one of those fake laughs that sets my teeth on edge. "I think some water went into my ears while I was showering. I still can't hear you." He tilts his head and shakes it as if clearing out the water.

I lean forward and when my mouth is a ten millimetres away from his left ear, I shout, "I am sorry, you annoying death-eater."

He jerks away and rubs his ear furiously, "How old are you, house-elf? Three?"

"House elves are nice," I defend. "They are small and hard-working and trusting."

Shriya Garg

"They are also ugly and slaves."

"Dementor!" I say angrily.

"Nearly Headless Nick," he counters.

I don't even have to think before answering, "Lucius Malfoy!"

"Bellatrix Lestrange," he taunts.

"Peter Pettigrew," I retort.

"Dolores Umbridge."

You must control your anger, I chant to myself. *You must control your anger. Just relax. Exhale. You can control your anger. In. Out. Don't let him get the better of you. Just relax.*

"BARTY CROUCH JUNIOR!" I say.

"Dudley Dursley!"

This is when I run out of names and look for something to beat him up with. I spot a cricket bat. It is heavy but I pick it up and wave it at him.

"Are you crazy?" he says, backing away. "Brawn over brain? I remember Vandana saying that nobody could defeat you in a verbal battle."

"Nobody can, minotaur. You just bring out the worst in me."

"There are no minotaurs in Harry Potter."

"Fine, then – Goyle!" I say and run after him.

He runs too but manages to shout over his shoulder, "Draco Malfoy!"

I climb on the bed to corner him and almost fall. I quickly balance myself again and we continue running in the living room.

"I already said that, Marvolo Gaunt."

"Pansy Parkinson," he mocks me again from the opposite side of the dining table. "Come get me," he sniggers, "if you can."

I crouch with the bat in my hand and look for an opening, "Lavender Brown."

He takes off again, breaks a vase but I do not stop. The bat is in my arms and above my head when somebody clears his throat in the doorway.

"I seem to have caught you at the wrong moment, Mr Khanna."

Three distinguished-looking men stand in the doorway with their briefcases and papers in hand. Both of us freeze. Aditya has one hand in front of him and the other behind, midway in the motion of running, and I know my hair is tousled and my hands up in the air, clutching the cricket bat. We must present a sight.

I slowly lower it and I know that I am blushing to the roots of my hair. That breaks the spell and Aditya straightens.

He strides forward to greet the guests and motions vaguely towards me, "Uh…she, she is my…new cricket instructor – Naina Kashyap."

I swallow audibly and put the bat down. I even manage to shake their hands without once meeting their amused gazes. Aditya takes them into his study and when he comes back, I say in a small voice, "I, I have to go. I'll see you later."

I try not to look at him but he captures my chin and grins, "It is alright. They are just some business acquaintances. I'd forgotten they were coming."

I push his hand away, "I hope you get fired."

"No, you don't. You came to apologise to me, remember?"

"Strangest thing," I say, faking some innocent surprise. "I seem to have forgotten." Then as if understanding is dawns, I nod, "Short-term memory loss. It is very contagious. I guess I should schedule an appointment with a doctor." I put on a faintly inquiring expression, "Which one are you seeing?"

Shriya Garg

Aditya blinks at me for a moment and then as my insult dawns, he starts laughing.

I smirk at him and turn to go. "*Definitely* funnier than you."

Naina Kashyap's Potential Suitor Victim #3
By Vandana Sinha
Name: Mukesh Lal.

Age: 26.

Occupation: Regional Sales Manager, Godrej Electronics, New Delhi.

Height: 5'7".

Weight: 81 kg.

Place of Ambush: Celini, Grand Hyatt.

Uniform: White *chooridar* with *jutis.*

Physical Appearance: Medium height, brown eyes, tanned and black hair.

Attractive Features(s): Has been very unlucky in love so far because he is rich *and* gullible. Has a good sense of humour.

Unattractive Feature: Is a health freak and eats out very rarely. Lives with his mother.

Spits sometimes when he speaks–

OPERATION TERMINATED.

"Naina, he only spits *sometimes*. You should at least go out with him once," Vandana says to me as we shop for Diwali at the Dilli Haat.

"Ugh, I am not going out with a guy who spits, sometimes or not." Without bothering to wait for her reply, I turn towards the shopkeeper to point to a brightly painted *diya*, "Yes, *bhaiyya*, show me this one."

"I thought so too," she said. "But time is running out and we need an alternative soon."

"Don't remind me of that. Dad has already begun the wedding preparations."

We buy the *diyas* and stroll around for some more stuff.

"You are coming to my Diwali bash, aren't you?" she asks as we buy two chocolate cones.

"Of course, why wouldn't I?"

"Well, Aditya is going to be there too."

"Oh, I forgot," I frown, remembering our last meeting. "He'd live, I guess. By the way, was he fired?" I ask and do not even try to disguise my hopeful expression.

"I am afraid not."

"That is unfortunate," I say in a tone that is comically dry. "Very unfortunate," I heave a sigh. "Anyway, how are things going between you and him?"

She shoots me a look from the corner of her eyes and a smile hovers on her lips. "If by that you mean if we have already slept together, the answer is no."

"That is not what I meant at all," I lie, letting out a breath that I wasn't aware I'd been holding. "But since you've already told me, why not?"

She looks at me oddly and sighs, "I don't know. He is

really nice and we have a great time together but something is lacking."

"Oh, really? What?"

"I don't know. Sometimes I think he is just taking me out because he is too busy to look for another girl."

"Oh."

"But I have a feeling he is going to be really good," she continues with her eyes twinkling. "I mean I have felt his chest. It seems really hard."

"It is," I blurt out and realise too late what I've done.

Her head snaps towards me, "How do you know?"

I quickly think of an excuse. I can't tell her of the day when I'd seen him shirtless. Yes, we are best friends and share everything but I don't think she would like hearing that I have seen her boyfriend shirtless when she hasn't.

The unfamiliar uneasiness which I'd felt when I'd seen his broad, broad chest comes back.

"Uh, when I'd pushed him in the bin, I felt it," I quickly reply.

She accepts that happily. *Why wouldn't she?* asks my guilty conscience. *It isn't as if you've ever lied to her before.*

"So, are your parents going to be there too?" I quickly change the topic.

"Where?"

"At your Diwali bash."

"Of course. They are the reason for organising the whole thing. That reminds me, do you think I should introduce Aditya to Mom and Dad?"

"Why shouldn't you?"

"As my boyfriend, I mean. They would be all over him and I don't think both of us have reached that level of relationship yet."

I shrug and absently hand out four ten rupees notes to the little children begging on the side-walk, "Your wish."

She walks beside me in thoughtful silence. "I think I'd just introduce him as my friend."

"Alright."

"So, are you going to come with anyone?" she asks.

I raise my brows, "I don't like your expression; reminds me of my great-grandmother who had only one eye and a dozen cats."

She ignores me, "Are you coming with a date? Diwali is going to be an ideal occasion for the inner Hindu woman in you to come out. You could bring Nitin."

I make a face. "Nitin is already seeing someone."

Her mouth opens in shock, "What do you mean?"

"Well, I called him up a couple of days to ask how he was doing after the injury and whether he wanted to get back again some time. He was distinctly uncomfortable and said that both of us are not that compatible and that he had actually already found somebody else…"

"The jerk."

"He was actually nice," I say.

"I bet that accident scared him away. I think Aditya told him of your previous date and what you'd done to him as well."

"So Nitin is now convinced that I come with an AK-47?"

"Nice choice of words. But yes, exactly."

"What do your parents have to say about these disastrous dates of yours?"

"They treat it as some inane habit of mine, which I am doing just to buy myself time. Mom asked me yesterday if I'd had enough and was ready to go through the photographs they had."

We walk in silence for a couple of minutes and finish our ice-creams.

Suddenly, Vandana stops walking, "That is an excellent idea."

"What?"

"Going through the photographs they have."

"What? No way!"

"Yes, way. See, our main obstacle right now is finding eligible suitors who qualify your rather difficult list and are interested in marriage."

She waits for my response, so I nod reluctantly.

"But the Ancients," she continues, making quotation marks with her hands in the air, "with their wide network of old aunties and gossiping grandmothers, don't have this problem. So you take a pick from their photographs, but meet him away from the house."

"Away from the house?"

"Yes, in a restaurant somewhere alone – not with his or your maybe future in-laws."

I mull it over, "I don't know."

"See the logic, Naina. This is the best option right now."

I think about it. "Oh, well, alright, but only because you say so."

"Come on," she says, taking my hand and dragging me to where her car is parked. "Let us check out the next one."

Naina Kashyap's Potential Suitor Victim #4

By Naina Kashyap (who is right now ignoring her sister's sniggers).

Name: Rishab Bisht.

Age: 27.

Occupation: Fashion photographer.

Place of Ambush: Vandana's house.

Height: 5'9".

Weight: 74 kg.

Physical Appearance: Quite tall, black-haired, brown-eyed and white skinned.

Uniform: Golden red and heavily embroidered *chooridar*.

Attractive Features: Page 3 material; is famous and more importantly, has a good reputation in the fashion world. Great sense of dressing.

Unattractive Feature(s): Is way too fussy with his clothes and sometimes likes to put on a little makeup.

Interests: Fashion trends, photography, clothes and beautiful women.

Atmosphere: Lively ambience with bright, joyful conversation.

Beware: Don't comment on his clothes – positive *or* negative.

His Ideal Woman: A beautiful woman with a svelte body, whom he can look at forever, and who shares his passion for ideal apparel for every occasion and thinks clothing means just more than just protecting the body against the weather.

"Are you finally ready to give up this insanity of yours or do you want me to pay more hospital bills?" my father asks just as I sit down on the dining table with my lunch. It was one of those national holidays when some great leader had taken birth (or maybe died, I don't remember) and everybody is home, having a late lunch.

I place my fork down, "I did agree to see one of the guys you chose for me."

He snorts and continues eating, not even bothering to look at me. "The youth of today…" he mutters to his plate and then turns to Uncle Sandeep for some support, "these matters of marriage are handled by experienced people like the elders."

Trapped, my uncle shoots me an uneasy glance and nods.

"If you want to meet Rishab," Dad continues, finally sparing me a glance, "the ideal way to go is for us to contact his parents, not you inviting him over."

My Mom looks at him angrily, "Let her do what she wants to, Jai. It is her life."

"Exactly," I point out.

There is complete silence. Nobody is even pretending to eat any more.

"You are only wasting your time," he says and puts the spoon in his mouth. "Already people are questioning what is wrong with us that we are allowing a headstrong 25-year-old girl to break all social norms and do what she wishes."

I try not to get rattled. "You said it: I am headstrong. And it is my life, so even if I do anything wrong, I won't blame you for it. This is not the 18th century any more when men didn't know that women have a brain of their own. I am not a girl any more. I have been voting for seven years. I would take Rishab to

Shriya Garg

Vandana's party and I don't care if you allow it or not." I push back my chair and get up, "And as for the bills, let me know the cost. I'll write you a check to cover the expenses."

Ignoring my mother's gasp, I go in and slam the door of my room. I am just 25, not some 35-year old spinster. And if old aunties have nothing better to do than watch those K-serials and gossip about the unmarried women in their locality, then it is they who need the medication; not me.

Since that particular discussion has killed whatsoever hunger I had, I look for something to distract myself with. Opening my laptop, I begin typing.

They found her in a dust-bin.

It was a stormy July night and the wind blew furiously over that particular section of the nation's capital. Torrential rain came and turned the already muddy, unmetalled roads into a wetland. The wind also did one more thing. It drowned out the sound of the three-day-old baby howling in the old dustbin, containing empty beer bottles and cigarette butts.

The man was in a hurry. He held his little son's hand and hurried across the empty street because he wanted to get home before they got drenched completely. When he heard the sound of weeping, he stopped.

"What happened, Daddy?" the little boy asked, looking up at his father who had suddenly stopped walking. He followed his father's gaze to the dust-bin ten feet away. "That is a dust-bin, Daddy," he provided helpfully in case his father had forgotten the strange object's name. "My teacher told me yesterday."

A knock on the door pulls me from the book. I get up and open it.

"What were you doing?" Ria asks, glancing quickly around her to see whether anybody has spotted her. Seeing the hallway empty, she pushes past me into the room and places packets from my favourite Chinese restaurant on to my desk. "I've been knocking for at least 15 minutes. Here, eat these."

I do not reply and settle down again.

Gathering his wits, the man hurried towards the bin and leaned in.

"My God," he whispered, seeing the little baby waving its clenched fist at the stranger. Its face was red from crying and the little chest heaved from the exertion. It was protected from the outside elements by a little blanket that was draped over the bin's lid.

"What are you doing?" Ria asks me, reading over my shoulder.

"You're still here?" I ask without looking up.

"Yes. Why aren't you eating anything?"

"I am not hungry," I reply absently, my hands flying over the keyboard. "I will eat when I am ready."

"Not when you are on your laptop, writing. You never remember anything then. What are you doing anyway?"

"I am writing a prologue for the book."

She gives a gleeful yelp, "Does that mean it is finally finished?"

"Almost," I said. "Now, leave me alone."

"This is your fourth novel, isn't it?"

I glare at her because she hasn't done what I've asked and then reply, "Yes."

"I have a hunch that this one would get published. It is your best work till now."

"Thank you. I wrote the other three because I wanted to. They were not exactly fit for publishing."

She opens one packet and hands me a fork with it. "Eat it as you write. Dad is so pissed off at you that he strictly forbade everybody not to hand you any food until tomorrow."

Shriya Garg

I finally drag my attention from the computer screen. "We have a McDonald's a block away," I point out.

"Exactly," she says and rolls her eyes.

"Thanks then," I say and dig my fork into one of the dim-sums. "Go now."

As soon as the door closes behind her, I put aside the bag.

"What happened, Daddy?" the child asked again, trying unsuccessfully to stand on his toes and peer in the bin. His father did not reply and instead looked around for a clue to find as to whom the baby belonged. When he saw the deserted street and not another soul in sight, he uttered a vile oath.

"Daddy!" the seven-year old boy gasped. "You said a bad word!"

But his father was too busy digging out something from the trash to pay him any attention.

So that the jagged ends of some of the broken glass bottles don't harm the little bundle in his hands, the man carefully manoeuvred the baby out. It howled again.

"It is a baby!" the child gasped again as understanding dawned. "It is a little baby!"

"Yes, dear," his father replied absently and looked down at the little bundle again.

"But what is it doing here?" the child asked.

"That," the man murmured, as he covered up the baby with blankets to save it from the rain, "is precisely what I am wondering."

The prologue done, I lean back in my chair and think.

As far as I can remember, I've always wanted to be a writer. I had prepared my first journal when I was five-years old. I wrote my first poem when I was six. When I turned 13, I started using complex English words that my parents couldn't pronounce. Due to this, I was often called the geek, the nerd, the bookworm and what not. I preferred to stay home and read a good book rather than go out and play. I am not bragging, merely stating same fact.

And when I had told my ambition to my father, he had given me a look of disbelief as though I had told him I wanted to become an astronaut. I was given one option: engineering. And when I rebelled, 'fine, do accountancy'.

So, I wrote for magazines, submitted a couple of articles to newspapers but that was, of course, just a *hobby*. Something to do to pass time; something I was to pursue after I got a decent job.

So, here I am. Through those back-breaking years of thick accountancy books and management courses, doing what I love to do, *and yet with no published material to my name,* I think derisively.

The idea for the book came one day when I was reading the newspaper. There was an article about how a local NGO had rescued 20 children below the age of 15 and employed as labourers in hazardous conditions in various parts of Delhi. They lived in slums, drank water from leaking pipes and had no access to any sort of education at all. The article, very well written, and certainly not the first of its kind, caught my attention. I am not ashamed to admit that I cried after finishing it.

Immediately, an idea struck and I opened their website and contacted them. They were gracious, helpful and absolutely delighted when they heard about the book. I interacted with them, saw them first-hand in action as they rescued children, who sometimes didn't want to be rescued and learnt that with the good part came the bad part too. Lack of funds, lack of co-operation from other civic agencies, children escaping from the shelters built especially for them, widowed mothers not willing to let go of their family's only source of income – the hurdles were many. But along with that was the light in those little eyes; their tears of gratitude, their surprise when they saw their bunk-beds, held a pen, wrote their first alphabet, got their first free lunch – all that more than made up for it.

Those two months when I accompanied the volunteers for research work had been very emotional for me. Newspapers and media can never truly convey their appalling living conditions. Not until you see a five-year old dying of common cold or a seven-year old child scavenging a rotten sandwich from the dust-bin with mosquitoes hovering above it right in front of your eyes do you realise how much you have always taken for granted. Food, filtered water, electricity, a soft bed, Mom's goodnight kiss, books, a football – everything we all have grown up with and never questioned.

That is what my book is about. It is the story of a young girl who was found in a dust-bin by a family and dropped off at an orphanage. Nisha escaped from the orphanage at the age of seven and what followed for her was a tough life on Delhi's streets.

After staring at the screen for half an hour more, I sigh and glance at the clock. It is just 5 o'clock, so I turn off my laptop and grab a coat. When writing doesn't help my mood, then only one other thing can.

"Oh, you've finally come, *didi*!" Seven voices chorus as soon as I enter the dilapidated park, three blocks down my house.

They are Ashish, Namrata, Sushma, Lakshmi, Karishma, Vibhay and Tanya – the children of local labourers who work at a construction site not far from there. None of them go to school because their parents don't have enough money, or do not want their healthy 11-year old children to waste six hours in school when they can work and contribute to the family income. Ashish and Vibhay work at a project which is being readied for the Commonwealth Games, and the rest of the girls are domestic helpers or serve tea in local restaurants.

Yes, despite the Right to Education being now a fundamental right, they still don't go to school. They hide whenever authorities come to check and beg pitifully when somebody – like me or local NGOs – threatens to report them. Their logic had seemed sound when their parents begged me with tears dripping down their noses: what would they do during the five-six years when their children are studying? Would education be helpful if they're already starved and nearly dead?

And they were right. They don't have a home to live in and their shanties are made of thrown-away plastic and brick stink. A family of four lives in the space which would only house my toilet. They are some of the worst-off families I've ever seen, but illiteracy would have only made them worse. So, we struck a deal.

I agreed not to report them, but in return, they would have to send their children for two hours to be taught by me. They were scared because they really thought I would report them to the authorities, and after knowing where they lived, they could not even hide. So they had to agree with me. I had hand-picked seven students who had basic knowledge of the English language.

This led us to where we are now.

I distribute the dozen pens and notepads I have with me and they quickly settle down on the hard blanket of grass.

"Let us begin by recalling our last week's 'Thought of the Week'," I say in a cheerful voice. "Who remembers it?"

Little Laxmi raises her thin, underfed arm.

"Yes, Laxmi?"

"Real knowledge is to know the extent of one's ignorance," (*reel no-knowledge is to know extinct of one's ignore.*)

"Yes, very good," I smile, give her a candy and prompt her further, "but who said it?"

She swells up with pride at my praise, but then a frown materialises between her pretty little brows. Laxmi is one of the brightest children I have ever met. Unfortunately, she doesn't know it. I can't even tell her because what help would it be to her except remind her that she cannot do anything with that brain of hers?

"Try to recall," I pat her hair. "I told you last week."

There is silence for a moment as everybody tries to recall, but no one, absolutely no one, tries to open their old copies which are lying in front of them and cheat. Unlike in a class, they know that they cannot deceive the teacher. As I have taught them for almost a year – even before the NGO, they know that I know their capabilities and they accept it for what it is.

"Confusion," Laxmi suddenly whispers.

"Yes, sweetheart," I say with a sad smile. "But it is Confucius. Come on, repeat after me, Con-few-shi-yus. C-o-n-f-u-c-i-u-s."

Taking their dull pencils in hand, everybody carefully writes what is told. My heart turns over at the thought of these little children's bleak future. If they had been born even in a middle-class family, they would have been future CEOs or managers; not housewives and plumbers. The unfairness of it all sometimes makes me want to cry.

"Now, who will explain to me what Confucius meant?"

Vibhay stands up, "Confusion – sorry, Confucius, meant that knowledge is not knowing everything, but rather knowing that you *don't* know everything." *(Confusion – sorry, Confucius, meant nolidge note nowing all, but nowing you don't know each thing.)*

I give him a candy. "Very beautifully put, Vibhay. Class, do you understand what he is saying?"

Everybody nods and then again scribble in their books. They have already written all this in their previous class but I do not try to stop them because they have the chance to write only once a week and I know for certain that they love working with their brains instead of their blistered hands.

Next I read them the latest chapter of my novel. What to teach them had posed a lot of problems in the beginning. I can't give them regular textbooks of every subject because they wouldn't have finished them by working only once a week. Thus, I concentrate more on their English and Maths rather than on Science or History. More importantly, I was worried about the medium of education. It turned out, though, that most of the children were from the north-east and south and knew more English than Hindi. So, I figured that if we could improve upon that, they can get employed in good homes and hence earn a better salary.

So, after reading one paragraph, I would ask one of them to summarise it, correct the deliberate errors I've made and then move on to the next paragraph.

An hour later, we begin with the tables and a little of multiplication and division.

In the last ten minutes of our session, I give them their thought of the week. "Kids, repeat this after me: Imagination is…"

"Imagination is…" they dutifully repeat.

"–more important than knowledge."

"–more important than knowledge," they chorus.

"–because knowledge is limited," I say.

"–because knowledge is limited…"

"–but imagination…"

"–but imagination…" they repeat again.

"–encircles the world."

"–encircles the world."

"Good. Now, do you want to know who said it?"

"Who?"

"Albert Einstein," I say slowly, giving them time to understand the alphabets I have used. "Who?" I ask.

"Alber E-i-…"

"Yes, yes, very good. But it is Al-burt Eiinstyne."

After a couple of more tries, we finally get it right. We learn its meaning and then I dismiss the class. None of the children leave though. We talk for fifteen to twenty minutes more. I give Karishma some money to buy new shoes even though she persistently refuses it and then tell Laxmi more about Albert Einstein. Then Ashish comes forward. A gangly boy of twelve with a sandy mop of hair, he carefully studies his shoes as he tells me that he has something to tell me.

I put aside Laxmi's question for a minute and turn to face him, "Yes, Ashish?"

"Me Mom let me go to school," he whispers to his feet.

The children around us fall silent. My heart contracts and I slowly walk to him: "Look at me, Ashish," I say gently.

He doesn't and I hear him sniffle.

"Ashish," I repeat.

He shrugs and wipes his eye with his shoulder. Finally, he looks up.

"Now say that again."

"Me Mom is sending me school. I will go school."

I nod. "Don't you like school?"

He furiously wipes away tears and jerks his head in a nod.

"Then why aren't you happy?"

"Then I will not come here."

Understanding the root of his misery, I crouch so that my eyes are on level with his, "You should be happy, Ashish." I lower my voice so that the ones who are so intently listening in can not. "You know how lucky you are? Your dreams are finally going to come true, sweetheart."

I wipe a tear away with my thumb, "I know you will miss us. And we'll miss you too. I'll miss you so much." His head shoots up at the last line, and I see something far more terrible than fear in those eyes. I see hope.

My composure slips then and I impulsively hug him. I feel tears sting my eyes; I am overjoyed, overwhelmed and sad all at once. And when I hand him my address and tell him to come to me if he *ever* needs anything, the tears gathering at the edge fall.

Then before I know it, he is hugging me back and both of us are laughing and crying at the same time. As his thin frame shakes under my arms with sobs that seem to be wrenched out of him, I wonder if anybody has ever said those words to the beautiful dark-haired child.

I do not think about it, I give him all the remaining sweets and bid others goodbye. As I open my car's door and get in, I hear some laughing and joyful exclamations coming from their corner.

I adjust the rear-view mirror and smile because I know what he has done. I know he has re-distributed those sweets among all of them and I feel so proud that my heart threatens to burst.

Education teaches people many things, but it can never teach anybody how to love.

"Best wishes, dear," my Mom says as she hugs Vandana on the doorstep of her house.

It is seven in the evening and we are the first guests to arrive at her Diwali get-together.

My whole family has come like her parents had indignantly demanded and I quickly ignore them to greet Mr and Mrs Sinha.

"Naina, you look so very beautiful tonight," Anushka aunty says.

I smile, "No more than you."

She gives me a playful slap on my elbow, "How can I compare with such vivacious youngsters like you?"

I grin, "There *is* no comparison."

She blushes, "You brat. But, really, I am serious. Where did you get this *chooridar* from?"

She fingers the hem of my stole, "You're just glowing in it with your skin and long dark hair."

"Oh, that suit isn't the reason why she is glowing," Ria teases and tips her head towards Rishab, who is standing right next to her.

"This is Rishab, aunty, the reason of my sister's smile."

Just so you know, Riya, the Queen of Cheesiness, reads romance novels for a living. "Ria," Rishab warns with a sheepish smile.

There is some ooh-ing and aah-ing as Vandana and her family examine him as though I have just bought him from the dog shelter.

"I am so sorry," I mutter to him from the corner of my mouth. "They are worse than my parents."

But he gives me a placating smile and shrugs, "Not your fault."

A squeal from the corner distracts us. Ria and Shaurya hence discovered the firecrackers.

"Look at this," Shaurya exclaims, pulling out a yellow cardboard box from the pile. "This gives out so much light…"

Ria doesn't hesitate and pulls out another, "And this is so loud…"

"Look at that." Shaurya says gleefully. "I have been looking for this everywhere! Ria, see…"

"Mr and Mrs Rude," I say with a meaningful look, "can't you at least *pretend* to be polite?"

"Oh, it is alright," Shashank uncle says with a dismissive wave of his hand. "I bought these for you children only. Go out and enjoy them."

"But eat something first," Anushka aunty insists.

"No, no, aunty, it is alright," Shaurya says, eyeing the lawn outside longingly.

"No, but I just can't allow it. At least drink something."

"Uncle," Ria aims her best charming smile, "we'll fend for ourselves. Won't we?" she asks Shaurya.

Their small tirade is interrupted by the arrival of other guests, all dressed up for the auspicious occasion and carrying gifts and hugging each other.

"Where did you get this pendant from?" Vandana asks, sliding next to me as we observe the commotion at the main door. "It is the prettiest thing I've ever seen."

I look around for Rishab, notice that he is suitably occupied with my father and whisper, "Rishab gave it to me."

Aditya enters the room then, carrying a big, wrapped package and looking as comfortable in an expensive *sherwani* as in a three-piece.

Vandana rushes forward to greet him and introduces him around. I turn my back on the couple and tap Rishab's shoulder.

"Hey," I say and lead him away from my father. "You are welcome."

"Thank you," he automatically replies at my sarcastic tone and after a pause, adds, "But for what?"

"For rescuing you from my father."

We both glance at him.

"Oh," he grins. I notice then that he too looks very handsome in his *sherwani*. The pale yellow colour, the red and white stones and the silky fabric reek of a designer tag and money. It certainly overshadows every other man's.

"I wish I could capture you right now," he says, touching my chin and observing me as I observe him. He tilts my chin at an angle, "You are more beautiful than most models I work with."

I shuffle my feet uncomfortably even though I know that what he is saying is not exactly the truth. Okay, far from it. "Thank you," I finally manage to force out.

"We have got to go out on a real date sometime next week. I am so sorry that we couldn't go out earlier," he continues, finally letting go of my chin. Another second and I would have had neck-pain.

"It is alright, I understand."

"I know you do," he smiles. "This month was very busy for me. Hopefully, I'd be free after tomorrow."

I nod in response and spot Aditya and Vandana heading towards us. His brows travel all the way up when he sees me in the traditional dress and then a lazy smile dawns.

I am not fooled even one bit. Just before they are upon us, I squeeze Rishab's hand and mutter, "Don't believe anything the guy says."

"Wow," Aditya says, giving me a slow and very insulting look. "You almost look…human."

I return his smile with a fake one of my own and subject him to the slowest perusal of history. "And," I say finally, with innocent surprise in my voice, "you almost look like a man."

He narrows his eyes.

"Almost," I complete my sentence, "but not quite."

He chuckles low in his chest and shakes Rishab's hand. "So you're the next poor victim then?"

"Poor victim?" Rishab asks.

Aditya shakes his head at me and in a tone of an adult scolding a three-year old for painting the walls, he says, "So you haven't told him yet, have you?"

I clear my throat meaningfully and smile widely, careful to hide my gritted teeth. Almost imperceptibly, I shake my head slowly to convey a no.

The expression on his face does not change as he turns to face Rishab and clasp him on the shoulder, "Thank God, we have New Delhi's biggest and best equipped hospital nearby."

Vandana whimpers and her head turns from me to Rishab and then to Aditya, like a ball in a tennis match.

"What are you talking about?" To his credit, Rishab looks only faintly curious.

I give Aditya a glare that could freeze molten lava. It does *not* stop him from opening his mouth.

Vandana wisely intervenes, "Don't be stupid, Aditya. Naina landing all the guys she dates in hospital is just a mere coincidence." She rings her hands desperately, "Don't give Rishab ideas."

"Naina did what?" Rishab asks, looking at me as if he's never seen me before.

I throw both of them a disgusting glance.

Shriya Garg

"Nothing, nothing. Ha! Ha!" Vandana laughs a little wildly in an obvious attempt to change the topic. "Oh, Aditya," she points to my neck, "look at what Rishab has got her! Isn't it the most beautiful thing ever?"

Aditya meets my eyes and doesn't even glance at the pendant when he answers, "Very."

I raise my eyebrows in amused derision but he breaks off the contact.

We proceed towards the table laden with drinks and snacks and I hear Aditya's chuckle beside me a scant second before I spot the reason for his amusement. "Look who we have here," he says to me and then, "hey, Ritesh! Over here, man. How are you?"

Ritesh spots both of us at the same time. He hears Aditya's 'hello', but pretends he hasn't and taking the hand of his mother, he leads her in the opposite direction.

"What happened? Why did the guy ignore you?" a puzzled Rishab asks Aditya.

"Oh, that," Aditya grins, "It's about something related to brown under-things and open zippers. You should ask Naina. She has a very interesting theory about that."

I roll my eyes and drag Rishab outside, "Come on, I told you not to listen to him."

"But why?"

I lower my voice to a whisper but not so much that it won't be overheard by anybody else. "Don't mention it, but he," I point my thumb towards Aditya *very* discreetly, "has a very delicate condition."

Rishab falls for it. He turns his neck just a little to get a glimpse of Aditya who is standing only a few feet away.

He lowers his voice too and with genuine curiosity, asks, "Delicate? *How*?"

Both of us turn again to catch a glimpse of him when Aditya notices us. He raises his brows in a I-know-you-are-up-to-something-bad-you-witch look and both of us hastily turn away.

I clear my throat delicately and pause to smile sweetly up at my audience. Vandana, who has followed us, looks very pale and I get into my role then, enjoying myself immensely. "You see," I begin with false reluctance, "when Aditya was little…" I break off and bite my lip. "Rishab, I don't think I should be the one to tell you this."

"Oh no, please do tell," Rishab begs.

I make a show of arranging the sleeve of the bodice of my dress just right. "When Aditya was very young…he…he was a witness to an…accident."

"Accident?"

Aditya takes a step forward and I hurry so that I can complete my story before he kills me. "Well, not accident, really. It was a murder."

I hadn't thought that grown men could gasp, but Rishab proves me wrong.

"One day when he arrived from school, happily gloating over the question he'd solved in school correctly for the first time, he saw a woman lying on his bed, her throat cut."

"Oh God!" Vandana says, too caught up in the tale that she forgets I am just making it up as she asks, "Who was she?"

"His neighbour's neighbour – "

Fingers clamp down on my forearm in an almost painful grasp. "You are a very good story-teller," Aditya says mildly, but I see the muscle twitching in his neck and I gulp.

"Uh, thank you."

"You almost had me believe that stupid tale myself."

"Stupid tale?" Rishab asks.

When Aditya awaits for me to clarify what he had said, I let out a sigh, mutter under my breath and lower my gaze to Rishab's shoes.

"I was just kidding, Rishab," I say.

"Well, that isn't nice," he replies, getting indignant. "You shouldn't have done that."

"Yes, I am sorry," I look into his eyes and try my best to look repentant.

"You don't sound sorry," Rishab observes, but he does not press the issue and when Vandana's mother announces that it was time for the fire crackers, we move outside to the lawn. Ria and Shaurya are throwing firecrackers at each other and laughing and shrieking. Predictably, Manya is trying to get them to stop doing that because there are other kids playing around who could get hurt and she fears that they would encourage them to do wrong things. Rishab and I join them and munch some chips and drink Cola before burning a couple of small, light sticks of our own.

Children are playing all around us and the whole area is lit up by candles because on Diwali, the festival of lights, it is said that Goddess Laxmi – the goddess of wealth – visits homes of her devotees and brings them wealth. So if the doors of the house are kept closed or there is darkness in the house, Laxmi wouldn't be able to enter.

A day earlier, the four of us had washed the whole house from the attic to the garage, collected a pile of clothes for donation and distributed gifts and sweets to friends, family and children who were not as fortunate as us.

Vandana had done the same to her house and the lights hanging from the trees add to the ambience of purity and festivity.

Rishab finally forgives me for the stupid joke inside and getting into the mood, even takes hold of my hand as we circle the perimeter of Vandana's housing society.

We had already talked on the phone a couple of times, so there is no initial awkwardness. He tells me about his workplace and I tell him about mine and we discuss our families. He is a single child who had nobody to play with in the neighbourhood. To pass time, he took to photography. His father is a journalist, so he had easy access to cameras and had a knack for using them. He tells me about the world of fashion, the fakeness, superficiality, greed but also the fame and glamour, which supposedly make up for it. He tells me of the 25-hour days of fashion schools and how sometimes he didn't sleep for three days continuously to complete a project.

Ria interrupts our discussion when she calls out to us to come over, "Hey, sister, come on, try this rocket."

Manya looks ready to throttle somebody, "Do you know that these bombs are made by little children in dreary warehouses in Shivakasi?"

Nobody bothers to reply to that and instead we turn to watch Shaurya.

An empty glass bottle is placed in the middle of the courtyard and he is lighting small *rockets* every couple of minutes, sending them swooshing over the terrace. When a rocket lands on the terrace of Vandana's surly neighbour, everybody laughs, except for Manya, of course. She makes a new resolution every year. She had resolved to protect the environment when she was just ten. While we used to stay up the night preceding Diwali, excitedly discussing the fire-crackers Dad had bought, she would stand in the first line of the parade with a banner screaming, 'Sun will Burn Your Skin and Bones, so Save the Layer Ozone. Say No to Fire-crackers this Diwali.' If that isn't the stupidest slogan ever, I don't know what is.

"Don't behave like a kid, Shaurya," she scolds him. "Have you any idea how harmful they are?"

"Watch," I lean over and whisper to Rishab. "Manya loves

76   *Shriya Garg*

the word harmful. Especially when she is lecturing."

"They could start a fire," she continues. "Do you see the children playing around? Do you have any idea how harmful they could prove to them? It is very callous to expose them to such heavy bombs at such a young age."

Rishab sniggers but tries to pass it off as a cough. Manya glances at him but does not say anything. "And do you have any idea, young man, how harmful this candle could prove to your dress? Quit laughing at me!"

"Sorry," Shaurya manages to mumble with a straight face.

"You are not seven any more."

"And you're not eighty already," the lawyer in him replies. "Come on, it's fun."

"Boys," she says in disgust and marches off.

"Haughty grandmothers!" he says to her retreating back.

"Oh, give it to me," I say before his mood can get worse and he spoils everybody else's too, because he is that kind of a man.

Despite my aversion to smoke and gunpowder used in firecrackers, I find myself caught up in the excitement of the children lighting them. The laughter proves infectious, and soon, I too am caught up in the fun to remember the health hazard.

We light a *chakri* which swivels round and round and throws sparks while making hissing noises. One of Vandana's mother's friends tries to cross the lawn just as we light a few *chakris*. She starts to jump up and down in order to dodge them and screams herself hoarse. We try to shout out a warning, but it is too late.

Fuelled by adrenalin, I start trying my hand at heavier bombs and firecrackers. So when Shaurya challenges me to take one of those harmless *bijli* bombs, which go off after a few seconds of lighting them to produce a lot of sound and little light,

I obviously do not refuse. The challenge is to keep the bomb in my hand and throw it in the air just before it explodes.

I tentatively take it in my hand and also a candle. Rishab tries to stop me because it is too dangerous but I frown at him and light it. A couple of seconds later, I throw it in the air where it bursts off beautifully. Boom! Mission accomplished.

"This is fun," I say.

"Do you know how much pollution it causes?" Manya sniffs, returning to observe us.

"Come on, sweetie, it is only once a year," I say but she doesn't reply. I am too far gone to care.

"Hey, give me another one," I call out to the boys, who are sitting guard on the pile of firecrackers so that they don't catch fire.

"Which one do you want?" one of them asks.

"Give me the one that gives out a lot of light when it bursts in the sky."

He gives me one of those cylindrical types which burst out into a beautiful pattern. I take it and place it in a corner of the lawn. I am wondering how to light it because I remember Shaurya doing something to the firecrackers before lighting them so that they don't combust immediately, but he is busy elsewhere. I look around but fail to spot Rishab.

Adrenalin can make people do very stupid things and that is the only reason I go forward and light the wick anyway. Predictably, before I can back away, it bursts into a loud noise. *Boom!*

For a second I am so disoriented that I only stare at the cloud of dust and leftover paper that is falling from the sky. I cough a little and somebody pats my back in reaction. Violently. I try to feel my fingers and toes and find that everything works fine. Someone pats my back again just as violently and I realise that I am not hurt, only because Aditya had pulled me away at the last moment.

"Will you stop hitting me?" I choke out.

"What the hell were you thinking, lighting it like that?" he shouts.

I flinch inwardly at his tone and try to move away from his tight grasp. His arm drops away and instead he shakes me till my teeth rattle.

"What are you doing?" I manage to shriek.

"What were *you* doing? Lighting it without removing the paper covering first? Do you know how seriously you could have been hurt?"

"Stop shaking me. Dammit! Oh, is that what I was supposed to do?"

He slams his hand against his forehead, "Naina, seriously, you should come with a warning sign: Beware – touch at your own risk!"

"Very funny," I say and look around. Everybody is looking curiously for the source of the explosion and I duck my head.

"Nothing happened, I am alright," I say to my mother, who keeps glaring at me from the doorway. "Thanks to Aditya."

"Thank you, son," Mom says to him, coming forward. She has the dazed look on her face that every female below the age of hundred and ten gets around him. Gushing at the sight of such a handsome hero coming to her daughter's rescue, she finally gathers her wits and finishes the sentence with, "for saving her life."

"Jeez, Mom, I wouldn't have died out there if Prince Charming hadn't come on his white horse to save me."

Aditya shoots me a glance and puts a comforting arm around her. My mouth drops open at such an atrocious gesture and I look around for Rishab. Shouldn't he be worried about me as well?

Aditya distracts me by grabbing my elbow. "What is it over there?" he asks.

I look at my elbow and see a minor scratch. "Gee, prince," I say, "it is just a little scratch."

"Let us get some ointment over it before it transforms into something more," he says firmly.

I protest but he doesn't listen. Vandana fetches him a first-aid kit and he guides me inside the house.

"Hey, it would look weird," I say, stopping him. "You are Vandana's boyfriend, not mine. It is alright. I'll find Rishab."

He looks at me oddly but continues dragging me into one of the rooms. "Rishab is nowhere to be seen. And what is with the word boyfriend? That's so high school? I am just putting some ointment, anyway; not making out with you."

"As if that is ever going to happen," I laugh.

"Yep." I sit down on the sofa and he knee down next to me. As he washes the wound with a towel, I realise something and say, "What is with you and these doctor things? I mean, first at Travertino's, when you knew all about how to keep the people away so that Ritesh could breathe and then now, with this ointment thing. I mean, how many guys do you know who would dash inside for medicine every time they were to get a scratch?"

He smiles and gently moves my arm to put the ointment. "I am from a family of doctors. Dad – general physician, Mom – a gynaecologist and sister is a neuro-surgeon at A.I.I.M.S."

"That explains it. Is your sister older than you?"

"Yep, she is going to be thirty-five next month. Happily married to another neuro-surgeon and has two kids."

"Wow."

"I know."

He wraps a white bandage around it and I sigh.

"What happened?" he asks.

"Nothing," I say thoughtfully. "I had figured that the first time a man would kneel in front of me, it would be because he was proposing; not wrapping a bandage."

He chuckles, "And you call yourself a feminist. Isn't it enough that the man is willing to become a slave for life? Kneeling and bowing to his master is just plain chauvinistic."

"Oh, come on." I say, "Don't you think it is romantic? A man – the epitome of power, health and vigour – bending for his fragile lady love."

He shrugs, "That answers it."

"Answers what?"

"Whether you believe in feminism or not."

I open my mouth to protest but he continues, "Anyway, I would find it romantic only if the woman kneeled to me and proposed."

"So, you're saying that you would never bend to a woman?"

"You think I am crazy? Never."

"You're just too macho for this scraping and bending, eh?"

"It is not about being macho. It is about having some sort of self-respect. This whole idea is ridiculous."

The bandaging is done and we get up, feeling awkward because this is the longest we have talked without fighting.

"We'll see. Maybe Vandana will bring you to your knees."

He laughs loudly, "I doubt that."

"Anyway, thanks for this," I add, waving my arm to indicate the bandage.

He clears his throat, "You are welcome."

Suddenly there is a knock on the door and Ria's voice calls out, "Naina, are you in there?"

"Yeah, come in."

"What are you two doing here?" she says and then must

have realised it was Aditya who was with me because she blushes.

"I was just putting some ointment over her cut before it gets worse," he says easily.

"That is right. I was coming to do just that myself," Ria says and her lie is so outrageous that my eyes widen.

He playfully ruffles her hair, "Wise kid. You should teach your sister that."

"I'd definitely try, but it is impossible to teach Naina anything," she says, with an expression of hero-worship in her eyes.

"Oh God, you two are so gross," I say. "Aditya, do you know why she agrees with everything you say?"

Aditya looks genuinely surprised. Hadn't he ever noticed that she always agreed with everything he said? Or was he so used to women throwing themselves at him and agreeing to everything he said that he didn't even notice it any more?

I am about to tell him about the Shahid Kapoor thing when Ria claps her hand over my mouth, her earlier concern about my cut forgotten as she pinches that very arm and drags me outside.

"You are such a jerk," she says as soon as we are out of earshot of a bewildered Aditya.

"And you are so pathetic. Just because his name is the same as Shahid Kapoor's in one of his hundred films, you'd worship the ground he walks on?"

"Naina, I'd worship the ground he walks on even if he was named Frankenstein. Silly, don't you see? The guy is what the Ancients would call a catch. He is drop-dead gorgeous, has so much brains that he can even fight you and survive and is well-off. He is caring – as you just saw inside – and he is strong and careful. He gets along with all three of your siblings – which is definitely saying something – and Mom already has a huge

Shriya Garg

crush on him. Are you so blind that you can't see what is standing in front of you?"

I am too shocked for a second to speak. And then sanity dawns. Blessed sanity. "What? Are you crazy? Ria, he is Vandana's boyfriend! I can't do that to her."

Ria curses, "He is obviously *not* her boyfriend. Have you ever seen them holding hands or even looking at each other more than with mild interest? He looks at *you* more than he looks at her."

I shake my head and start to move towards the main door, "His name has obviously clouded your thinking. When you're thinking straight again, talk to me, otherwise don't."

I am about to make a graceful exit when Rishab stops me in my way. "Naina," he says anxiously, "I have been looking for you everywhere. I heard you were injured in an accident with a firecracker – are you okay now?"

I am touched by his concern but I wave it aside because Ria's words are still roaring in my ears.

Handsome? Rishab is handsome. He also has brains because he has made it big in the fashion industry, plus he is caring and gets along with my family quite nicely.

The fighting-me-and-still-surviving part? Well, unlike Aditya, I do not dislike a person so much on sight that I start fighting him. Maybe a couple of years down the lane, when we would be living happily married in a little house in South Delhi, Rishab would scold me for the phone bill. Then we'd see who survives it.

"Of course I am okay," I reply. "It was just a scratch. I got it bandaged."

He pats the bandage and nods, "Good, these little cuts can turn very nasty if left untreated."

I smile in response and we shift to the dining room for dinner.

The dinner turns out to be a lively affair with at least a dozen predictable North Indian dishes and some non-predictable ones, with even more kinds of desserts.

"Really, Anushka, you shouldn't have gone to so much of trouble," Mom tells Vandana's mother when she comes to know that the food hasn't been provided by a caterer.

"Oh no, it was nothing," Mrs Sinha says. "Vandana helped me with it."

Mr Sinha picks up his glass of wine, "On which other occasion would you cook, if not on Diwali?"

"My! Vandana, you know how to cook?"

"A little, aunty," Vandana replies and shoots me a smug smile. I give her an evil one in return. She knows what would happen if she continues down this line.

My mother doesn't notice Vandana's groan because she is already too busy giving me disapproving looks. "This Naina, I tell you," she shakes her head and turns to Mrs Sinha who is sitting next to her. "She doesn't even know how to light the stove."

"Not true! I can make Maggie," I protest.

Mom gives me another disapproving look and then looks fondly at Vandana. "Vandana dear, you should really teach your friend something. No wonder her past few attempts at finding a suitable husband have been such a disaster. Don't you agree, Nandini?"

I cough loudly to indicate that this subject is not to be discussed in front of Rishab and Aditya and all the other eligible bachelors roaming around but, *of course* everybody ignores it.

"I am absolutely in agreement with you, Shivani," Aunt Nandini says. "Even Manya doesn't know anything about cooking or any other household chores for that matter. At your age, I used to manage all my five little sisters and cook the evening meal daily."

I cough even louder but except for Aditya who shoots me a devilish grin as he stares at all the mothers with fascinated attention, there is again no reaction. It is amazing how much of a deaf ear a certain person can develop when he puts his mind to it.

"Who will marry a woman who cannot even make tea without burning it?" Mom asks the table in general in a tone one might use for a kid, *What will happen now that the whole world has been destroyed by aliens?*

"I tell you, Rishab, son, I never wanted to say this but you would definitely have to hire a cook after your marriage with my daughter – Naina, sweetie, are you choking on something?" Mom adds innocently.

I press the back of my hand to my mouth while my eyes start watering. Ria begins to fan my face vigorously with her hand. The discussion continues.

"Oh, aunty," Rishab replies gamely, "it is alright. I know how to cook."

I choke even harder. *After marriage? Hello, we met, oh I don't know, like an hour ago?*

There is a collective gasp around the table and even Aditya widens his eyes and puts his hand over his mouth, when I know for a fact that he has no idea why the others have gasped.

"Oh no, son, you are the man in the house," my father interjects, glaring at me as if it is my fault. "You cannot do the cooking."

"Oh, uncle, it is the twenty-first century now. Certainly there are no misconceptions of the sexual division of labour any more. I mean, Naina obviously would continue working after marriage, so when she has a share in the household income, which is, according to orthodox beliefs, my job, then why shouldn't I share the household chores which are again the woman's job?"

Everybody reacts to his outpour of English language differently. The elders look down at their food with odd, embarrassed smiles as if Rishab is too young to mean what he is saying. Vandana, I, Ria and Manya look at him with gratitude and Shaurya and Aditya have disgusted looks on their faces.

"But at least Vandana's husband would have an easy job of it," Anushka aunty finally says to break the tense silence that has settled over the table.

Vandana blushes while Aditya continues eating like he is not related to the person being talked about.

"Vandana, tell me, what all can you cook?" Dad asks, ignoring my glare.

With every type of cuisine Vandana rattling off, all the youngsters at the table look at her with varying degrees of horror. Aditya's eyebrows disappear in his hairline. Really, who would want to waste so much of time in the kitchen when takeout is just a phone call away?

After the somewhat uncomfortable dinner, the men retire to Sinha uncle's study for drinks and cigars and a game of cards while the women retire to the master bedroom for their stuff.

The children – us – wonder what to do and in the end go for a walk around the swimming pool, which is on the other side of the apartment complex.

"Did you really mean what you said about sharing the household chores?" I ask Rishab, as we trail a little behind the whole group.

He takes my hand and replies, "Of course. I am comfortable enough in my skin. Thus cooking does not seem like a threat to my masculinity."

Shaurya and Aditya, who are walking ahead of us, stop because they must have heard his statement. I squeeze Rishab's hand to warn him of the danger but he is not paying me any attention. "I mean, why else wouldn't a man cook at home?

Shriya Garg

Look at all the famous restaurants, the chefs are mostly male. Our gender is comfortable with cooking if it gives monetary returns but at home, we are willing to let…"

"Uh, Rishab…" I say uneasily, seeing Aditya and Shaurya first look at each other and then fold up their sleeves.

"…our womenfolk toil first their brains at work…"

"…Rishab…" I tug at Rishab's *kurta*.

"…and then go to the kitchen…"

"…Please don't…"

"…and fix us dinner. That is just so…"

"Rishab! Help, I am falling," I scream. I stand at the edge of the swimming pool, facing it backwards and pretend to fall just to make him stop talking. That grabs his attention and as he walks forward to save me, I see Aditya, Shaurya, Manya and even Vandana stride forward too, with the same intention.

I pretend to clutch the empty air around when falling backwards and Rishab grabs my hand with both of his. Unfortunately, the force of his hold is so much that it disrupts my balance. Before I know it, I really begin to fall, and along with me, Rishab too.

Somehow, our positions get reversed and he lands into the pool first, with a hearty *splash*.

Fortunately, I am rescued at the last minute by a firmer, stronger hand capturing my wrist. I hang on to him like my lifeline, and let go of Rishab's grasp.

"My branded clothes!" Rishab screams as he lands in water and I stand unharmed at the side, my hands tangled in Aditya's.

"Oh my God," Rishab screams again, his head going underwater every couple of seconds so that the sentence comes out as "O my – *(gurgle)* – od."

"It is alright," Aditya calls out. "Your clothes can be…"

"No, no! I don't know how to swim. *I don't know how to swim!*"

I remove my hand from Aditya's as he runs forward to save him.

"Please, help me," Rishab shouts and my heartbeat triples. "*Help me, I am drowning. I cannot swim!*"

Suddenly Aditya stops running so that Shaurya, who is right behind him, bumps into him. Both of them stand there, smiling for some reason.

"Save him," I say, wringing my hands. "Shaurya, *please,* go and get Rishab."

Rishab raises his hands over his head and keeps disappearing underwater.

"Oh my gosh, he is drowning. Shaurya! Aditya!" Vandana screams too.

I quickly divest myself of my sandals. Aditya looks at me and rolls his eyes.

"Rishab," he calls out in a clear voice just as Manya is also about to dive. "Chill, man, the pool is only five feet deep."

I stop trying to get my darned footwear off. Manya's mouth falls open.

Rishab, on the other hand, keeps struggling for another second before he realises what has been said. "What? The pool is only…" he stops thrashing his legs around and stands up, so that the water comes only to his neck. "I can stand…oh…the pool…I thought…" he mumbles, looking at his hands and touching his face to check if he is really alive. There, painted on the side wall, we all see, is written in yellow: *Maximum depth – five feet.*

"Rishab? You okay?" I call out, throwing both the other guys a disgusted look for the fun they are having at the cost of my date.

"Yeah…I'm okay…I think…But I really thought…"

"Let us get you out of there," I say. "Ria, go quickly, get a towel."

It is October when people hardly swim, so there isn't even any lifeguard around. Why was the pool full of water then? I don't know. I just cannot understand how nobody except Aditya and Shaurya notice the depth sign. *Karma*, I suppose.

But Ria is not listening to me because Aditya starts laughing. Then Shaurya and Vandana join him and pretty soon everybody except me and Rishab are laughing.

"What is so funny?" I ask them with my hands on my hips. Rishab is struggling to come out of the pool with his heavy clothes which have become heavier with the water.

"You must," Manya points out. "You dismembered your date again."

"At least we haven't had to take him to the hospital…" Aditya manages to say through his laughter when the weight of his heavily embroidered cloth with the added water proves too much for Rishab and he collapses in an awkward heap as soon as he touches solid ground.

"Ow," Rishab says. "I think I have hurt my ankle."

"…yet." Aditya completes his sentence.

Beep. Beep. My phone rings and I sleepily thrash my arm out towards the side-table where I usually keep it.

"'lo?"

"Naina?" Vandana's voice gasps at the other end and I try to sit up.

"Yes? Vandana, what happened?" I say, flipping on a light to check the time: 12:30 p.m.

"Naina, Aditya and I broke up," Vandana's soft vulnerable voice confesses in a whisper.

My drowsiness evaporates.

"He did *what*?"

"You heard it! We broke up just now. I'd invited him to my place for a late dinner when he said it."

"But *why*?"

"I don't know," her voice shakes a little. "I can't think right now."

"Do you have any chocolate?"

"I don't know…I think so."

"You need to hold yourself together, honey," I say gently, getting up and into a jeans and T-shirt. "I would offer you my shoulder but I am going to be too busy burying the piece of dirt you dated."

"Naina, it is not his fault."

I hold the phone in place with my shoulder as I tie my laces. "You needn't defend him. I know you, and he just cannot dump you and walk away as if nothing ever happened."

"Naina! Forget it, the guy is history."

"Not yet but would be as soon as I find Manya's gun."

"Naina," she laughs shakily. "What the hell are you thinking of doing? It is the middle of the night."

"You said he just left your house."

"You're crazy," she says. "And I love you so much for it, but you still cannot go to his house. At least not right now."

I sit back to think. Mom and Dad would go crazy if they see me leaving at this time of the night. "Much as I hate to admit it, you're right." Then I brighten up, "But there is always tomorrow."

"Naina, you won't."

"Don't worry," I assure her. "Of course I would."

Still 19 October even though it is a different day which is coincidentally also going to be the Last Day of Aditya Khanna's pathetic existence

"Manya, can I borrow your gun for half an hour?" I ask her as soon as she gets back from her shift which is at about 8 at night.

She chokes on the water she is swallowing, "May I ask why?"

"Sure. I got to beat a guy."

"Why?"

"He dumped a friend of mine."

"Aditya?"

I raise my eyebrows, "I have other friends, too."

She laughs, "Yeah. Right. Sorry, no gun."

"I knew it! You people have this ridiculous love for this guy. You don't know his dark side. In front of everybody he is nice and handsome and charming and as soon as you turn your back, the *basilisk* in him comes out."

"Naina, just listen to yourself. You're crazy while Aditya is amazing. He is the only person I've ever met who listened to the whole story of my last case and even offered a suggestion at the end."

"That is not true. I listen, too, when you speak."

"So why were your eyes closed the last time when I had to shake you to wake you up?"

"That? Oh, that was because I was just thinking about what you'd said."

She raises her brows and I add defensively, "What? I think *very* deeply."

"Forget it; you're not getting my gun. You don't even know how to hold it."

"I am not going to *use* it! You can even take out the bullets. I just need it to scare him. This is going to be an example for all

92   *Shriya Garg*

the boys who use girls just to get what they want and then discard them like toilet paper."

"Awh, Naina, I am sure Vandana and Aditya have not slept together."

"True, but he would have. Wait, how do *you* know that?"

"It is obvious from the way they touch each other," she replies in her I-am-so-wise voice. "That particular level of intimacy shows."

I arch my brows, "You seem to know a lot about such things, *little sister*. But I won't ask you further about it because, hey, I at least, am such a good sister. And this is why you're also going to give me the gun."

"No! Use something else if you really have to beat him up, I guess. Naina, I hope you know that the guy can beat up three of you with one of his hands tied."

I let out a deflated sigh, "I know."

"Then?"

"I am counting on the element of surprise and the fact that he doesn't hit a woman."

"Uh…best of luck, then."

"Thanks," I say, trying to appear confident as I move to grab a crowbar that comes to my waist-level from the tool-shed.

Half an hour later, I knock on his door. Though I know that blasting through it, shouting *"Delhi Police! You are under arrest!"* would have made a more impressive entrance, but some people (*read:* Manya) just don't have a sense of humour.

Aditya opens the door (sans a shirt), sees me standing with a crowbar poised to fight, rolls his eyes and closes the door on my nose.

"What the…?" It takes me a moment to realise that he has closed the door on me. *Me.* Naina Kashyap.

"Go away," he says from the other side. "I can't open the

door to you without my bullet-proof vest – which is now also water-proof."

He chuckles at his joke and I growl, "Laugh all you want but always remember Manya Kashyap's gun."

The sound of laughter stops and the door is opened carefully. He crosses his arms and leans a shoulder against the door.

"I guess you *had* to come and make my day, right?"

"That was my best friend you dumped, you shallow jackass!" I say, poking him with the tip of the crowbar.

"Hey, keep that thing away, it *hurts*. And I didn't dump your best friend. We mutually agreed to part ways."

"Oh, is that what you think?" I reply, still poking and dodging his fingers as he tries to take my weapon away. "Isn't this what they all say?"

"No, that is not what they all say. The relationship wasn't going anywhere."

I get tired of the crowbar that never seems to hit its target, so I throw it away and punch Aditya Khanna's stomach right there on his doorstep, where any one of the forty-two people living on his floor could have seen it. There is a sound of something breaking and then, "Ouch, omigosh, *ouch!*"

"Naina, it is alright. Show me your hand."

"I think you've broken my bone," I shout.

"I am sure it is not broken. Wait – *I* broke it? *Excuse me…*"

"Ow, ow, ow!"

"I almost feel sorry for you," he says as he gently takes my hand and ignoring the killer glare I shoot him, leads me inside from the prying eyes that have stopped on their way so as not to miss even one scene of the unfolding drama. "Almost, but not quite," he continues, throwing my words back at me. "At least, this time I don't have any business associates who are going to turn up."

"Can you please wear a shirt?" I blurt out.

"Why?" he glances down at his bare – correction: fantastic *and* bare – chest and grins, "My incredible muscles do something tingly to your stomach?"

How right, I think.

"How wrong," I say.

"I like it this way," he says. "The suits are too confining to wear all day."

"Whatever. I have seen too many naked chests to care, anyway," I wave my hand in the air to indicate my '*whatever*' but it throbs and I remember that he has broken it.

"I bet. So shall we have a look at your hand?"

"By all means," I say through gritted teeth. "After all, it is you I have to thank for this splendid piece of ill-formed hand."

"Does it really hurt?" he asks and the trace of amusement in his voice recedes a little.

"A little," I say.

He feels my knuckles and presses them once or twice and finally announces, "No broken bones. I think some ice will do the trick. You shouldn't have messed with my abs."

I look down at his abs and then quickly look up because he is Aditya Khanna, the man who dumped my best friend and made my life hell.

"Where is the crowbar?" I ask.

"Somewhere outside the front door. Why?"

"I brought it for a reason."

He goes towards the kitchen and takes out an ice tray from the freezer. Slapping the tray against the sink, he puts the cubes in a clean cloth that is hanging from a wooden peg and helps me sit on the marble counter. Then taking the packed napkin, he presses it over my hand.

"Tell me," he says conversationally, "have you always been this disaster-prone?"

"Um, no, not always."

"I really think that you can keep all the hundred something hospitals of Delhi running single-handedly with your victims."

"Not true."

"Okay, maybe not exactly, but I am not that far in my estimation."

"You know," I say, "now, when I think about it, I seem to have become this accident-prone ever since I first met you. Remember the Ritesh incident?"

He laughs and continues pressing the ice, "Oh my God, the look on your face when he stammered, '*S-s-skin un-under-underwear*' was priceless."

I laugh as well and shake my head, "Jesus, no, it was awful. I was sure that I'd killed him."

"Me, too. And Nitin? Oh God, the way he sang…"

We laugh harder. "But he was cute. Did he find any nice Indian girl, by the way?"

"I think so. We have been a little out of touch since that incident. He found out that I had set him up on purpose."

"You are horrible," I criticise him.

"I wanted revenge. Setting you up with him seemed the ideal solution."

"But it was a great day. I pushed you in that garbage bin, remember?"

"Vividly," he replies darkly. "That was my favourite shirt, you know."

"Even better," I say with a satisfied smile.

We sit in silence for a couple of seconds before I suddenly groan out aloud.

"What?" he asks.

I cover my face with my hands and groan even louder. "We were acting like friends! We!"

He sounds pretty surprised himself as my statement sinks in, "Wow. You are right. Angelina Jolie and Jennifer Aniston kissing each other," he murmurs.

"I get to be Jolie," I immediately reply. "You can be Aniston."

He shrugs, "I do not exactly fantasise about being any of these women."

"I can understand."

"Let us change the topic. So, how is Rishab?"

"Hairline fracture," I say and make a face when he laughs. "If you could have rescued him sooner, this wouldn't have happened."

"He went out with you. Of course, he *had* to land up in the hospital. And if I had rescued him, we would have missed the entertainment. It was priceless. In the next party we go to, I am going to erect a booth outside – fifty rupees for the drama. Quickest way to become a millionaire."

"A moment of peace," I say to the ceiling, "and then that mouth."

He throws back his head and laughs.

I ignore it, "Do you know that he is hydrophobic?"

"Well, that would certainly cure it."

"I could not believe it when you and Shaurya just stood back and smiled when I honestly thought he was drowning."

"I don't like the guy but that doesn't mean I would have let him die," he says and then falls silent. "Correction: *most* probably I wouldn't have let him die."

"You are unbelievable," I say.

"Speaking of unbelievable, do you know that when Vandana told me that you're an accountant I thought she was pulling my leg?"

"I wish."

"What?" he looks up from where he is observing my hand. "You didn't want to be an accountant?"

"Are you serious? Of course, I didn't."

"Then why?"

"I wanted to be a writer. In fact, I still want to be a writer but my father was adamant against journalism. A woman travelling all around for news? No way that *that* was going to happen in the Kashyap family. He refused to listen when I explained that journalism was not just roaming around with a mike and cameraman in tow."

"You could have still done some writing course. There was no need to be an accountant."

"Well, actually, he wanted me to do engineering. Always been his big dream and all that. But I dug in my heels then. I hated science. What about you? Why did you become an engineer?"

He smiles and instead of answering my question, removes the compress, "Want a drink?"

"Coke."

I take the one he offers with my uninjured hand and watch him open his can.

"I always wanted to be an engineer," he replies to my earlier question. "I loved to open things and check them out. By the time I was five, I'd already graduated from telephones to my Dad's CPU. In eleventh, I naturally opted for Science because Chemistry and Physics were my best friends."

"Yours?" I interrupt. "Oh tell me another one."

"Yeah, mine. And no, I am not lying. I was one of those typical geeks whom everybody ignored because he was always unaware of what was happening around him."

"But I always imagined you to be the sort of guy who used to fail till Class X and then in Class XI, suddenly lost all interest in his dozen girlfriends and cars and turned to Science and Maths."

"Far from it. I hadn't had any girlfriend till I did my M.B.A."

"Are you serious?" I ask, my mouth dropping open.

"Very."

We move towards the sofa and continue talking.

"So, what type of books do you write?" he asks.

"Well, I explored the various nuances of writing by trying out different genres. I even wrote a para-normal book – science fiction – fantasy."

"And?"

"And I realised that it was not my thing."

"Wait – do you like Chetan Bhagat."

"Whenever I am in mood of light read, I pick him up. Usually I go for heavier stuff."

"Harry Potter?" I tease.

"No," he grins, "I liked *The Kite Runner*."

"Wow, really? I loved *The Kite Runner*."

"The best book ever," he says.

"The best," I agree, "after *Harry Potter*."

"Of course."

"Did you like *A Thousand Splendid Suns*?" I ask.

"A splendid book. Some say it is even better than Khaled Hosseini's first book. I tend to agree."

"No, *The Kite Runner* was better."

"If you say so."

"Tell me about your book."

"What? You really want to know?"

"Very much."

"Oh, if you insist," I say happily and tell him the whole plot. "The one I am working on right now, is the story of a young girl who is found freezing in a dust-bin. She is picked up by a man who is passing by but later is given to an orphanage from where she had escaped at the age of…"

An hour later, his phone rings and I notice the time. "Oh my God," I say when he comes back. "Manya was right about you."

"About me?" he asks.

"You are a very good listener. I never noticed how the time flew." I look down at his shoes, "I am so sorry. You must be bored to death."

He looks at the clock. "No, are you crazy? I never noticed the time either. You are an amazing story-teller. I just can't understand why you haven't had your book published yet."

"I do. It seems that whenever I am sure I have added the final touch, I get struck by a new idea to twist the plot which is simply brilliant and I have to put it in the book. But for that, I have to edit at least fifty pages and on and on this process continues," I say glumly.

He pats my hand sympathetically, "It happens. Would you mind terribly e-mailing me the book?"

My head comes up, "You're saying it just to make me feel better."

"No, I swear. I love your plot. It is different, and the message is subtle but very effective."

"Thanks."

"Have you been writing long?"

"Ever since high school," I say.

"Some perseverance," he replies.

"Not like yours. I mean, IIT – Wow! You must be some genius."

"Not genius – Nah. I merely liked it, so I threw myself into it. It seemed thrilling to me at that time."

"Not any more?"

"No," he confirms. "After I discovered beer and women, Physics lost its appeal."

"Yeah, you really don't look like a geek."

We share a smile and then he gets off the couch. "You want some dinner? It is late."

"Oh no! I really need to start back for home as it is very late."

"Not without dinner," he insists. "Come on, it would be fun. You could help me."

I laugh, "Have you already forgotten?"

"Oh, sorry, you don't know how to cook. Come on, that seems impossible."

"Actually Mom was exaggerating; I know how to turn on the stove. You know those automatic ones in which you turn the knob and the flare comes on."

He raises his eyes towards the ceiling in mock despair, "I should have known."

"But you know how to cook?"

"Yep. I lived in New York for three years. It was a do or die situation?"

"Then why did you have such a disgusting look on your face when Rishab talked about sharing household chores?"

"I didn't like him speaking for the whole of our gender. It seemed presumptuous. So, you are staying?"

"Oh, no, I really have to go. My parents are going to kill me once I get home."

"Here, let me talk to your Mom," he says, taking out the cell phone. "What is the number? Wait, I have it in here."

"Please don't. Mom would definitely agree because you are an eligible bachelor and I am an old spinster and when I get home, I would have to face the firing squad. Plus, everybody knows that we hate each other's guts, so they are going to be doubly curious."

He looks at me curiously. "We don't hate each other's guts." He pauses. "Do we?"

"I came here with a crowbar to kill you or at least fracture some of your bones – Shit! I forgot all about that."

"All about what?"

I look at him angrily. "That you're a monster who made my best friend cry."

"Aw, shit, Vandana cried because of me? Seriously? I did not know that; I am sorry," he looks so genuinely upset that I am tempted to believe him, but I persevere.

"What did you think she would do when her boyfriend dumped her? Dance to *Hips don't Lie?*"

"Naina, I told you," he says slowly, as if explaining the Pythagoras theorem to a seven-year old. "We mutually agreed to part ways but remain friends."

"Just a second," I say holding up my hand. "Answer me honestly. Was it because of me?"

"Was what because of you?"

"The reason you dumped her?"

"Oh, you silly girl, of course it wasn't because of you. And I am saying this for the last time that both of us agreed that this relationship wasn't going anywhere."

"I finally believe that you didn't know about the opposite gender till graduation," I say, glad that it isn't because of me that my best friend is so upset. "Think about it, Aditya, would Vandana have a choice but to agree after you tell her you intend to dump her?"

"Is anybody listening to me here?" he asks. "I didn't dump her! She was the one who brought up the topic."

"Yes, why not? Wait, what?"

"Now you are listening."

"You didn't dump her?" I ask uncertainly.

Shriya Garg

"Congratulations for finally getting it right. No, I did *not* dump her. Yesterday night, she brought up the topic herself. Said that there was no spark between us and we were too old to play. She is looking for someone to settle down with and was wasting her time with me. If anybody should be the injured party, then it should be me, not her."

I stand up, "But she called me up last night and said that you broke up with her."

"I did. In the end, I agreed to what she said and that was we should break up."

"But she was crying!"

"Why would she cry?" he asks. "Are you sure she was crying?"

I think back to the previous night. The details are groggy but I am pretty sure she was upset.

"She sounded sad," I say.

"Of course, she would be sad. We wasted almost a month on each other."

"Oh, maybe you're right."

"Thank you," he says angrily. "So now you want the dinner? I am going to ask the guy to deliver Chinese."

"What? Takeout?"

"You spoiled my cooking mood with your chat."

"Then I don't think I should stay. You eat; I'll go."

He takes my hand – the uninjured one even though the injured one is pretty much cured – and pushes me down on the sofa.

"Sit," he orders. "And wait while I talk to your father."

I wisely keep silent as he waits for the line to connect and then watches in surprise as his whole face changes. "Hello, Manya? Hi, sweetie, it is Aditya here. Can I talk to your Aunt Shivani? What? She is not there? Oh, then your uncle – Oh! Wow, really?

That is sad. So when would they return? Oh, okay, so do you mind if Naina stays over for an hour for dinner? Thank you and keep all your doors closed, okay? No place is never too safe. Yeah, 'bye, honey! Goodnight."

"What was that?" I ask horrified.

"That was Manya," he says casually. "Lovely girl."

"Manya talked to you like that?" I put my hand under my chin and close my mouth.

"Yeah, she seems way too gentle for a cop. Anyway, as it turns out, some distant aunt of yours in Faridabad has had a heart attack and all the four elders have gone there. Shaurya is on guard duty and they have promised to be back by tomorrow."

"Wow, must be serious. Oh my God, Aunt Usha! Oh, no," I say and take out my phone to call Mom.

"Give me a minute," I say.

"Sure," he nods and takes his own phone to order the food.

"Hey, Mom," I say as Mom picks up her phone, "What happened to Aunt Usha?"

My Mom's voice reflects my worry. "Heart attack, honey. We wanted to reach her before it is…" her voice shakes and Dad comes on the line.

He clears his throat,. "We wanted to reach her before it was too late," he completes the sentence. "We'll let you know the outcome by morning. Take care of everybody else, sweetie."

Before I can tell him that I am not at home and at Aditya's, he disconnects.

"How is your aunt?" Aditya asks, handing me some more Coke.

"Not good," I say sadly. "Look, I am not in the mood for food. Is it alright if I go home?"

He thinks for a second, "Alright, but are you sure you'd be able to drive?"

"Don't be stupid, I'll manage. In case you have forgotten, it is not me who has had an attack."

"No, I don't think so. What sort of a man would I be to allow you to drive back alone at this time of the night with one hand?" When he sees me objecting, he inserts, "Humour me, alright?"

"Okay, but what about your dinner?"

"I'll cancel it."

"Wait, it is okay. We can wait till the time it gets here. You eat it and then we'll go."

"Are you sure won't mind?" he asks.

"Of course. You shouldn't miss your dinner because of me."

He shrugs, "Great. The guy said to wait for twenty minutes. Why don't we watch some movie for the time being?"

"Alright."

He finally dons a shirt and then leads me to the video rack. "Which one do you want to see?"

"You pick. We are not going to watch the whole of it anyway."

"Hm…you like *Home Alone*?"

"It's cute."

"Then that is it. Let me get some popcorn while you put in the CD."

So, as it happens, we turn off most of the lights and sit down on the same couch because we have to share the popcorn.

Mid-way through the movie, the bell rings, and we jump because we had forgotten all about dinner. We pause the video as he pays the delivery man and brings the food in the paper boxes in which it has come. We begin to eat directly from them.

"I thought I wasn't hungry," I say, dipping a dimsum in the red sauce, "but turns out I am."

He looks at me and his face is in shadows because the only illumination is from the TV, but I still see him grin. He does not say anything.

The movie ends but we are in mood for some more and there is still some leftover food to finish. So we put in *Home Alone 2* and continue laughing.

Midway through *that* movie, the previous sleepless night and the strain of Aditya and Vandana's break up and Aunt Usha's heart attack begin to show its effect on me and I start feeling drowsy. I feel uncomfortable in the cramped couch but I do not want to keep my head on his shoulder – boy, don't even go there – so I do not move it. No way am I going to use him for my comfort. I am better than that.

An hour later, I wake up half-sprawled in his lap.

"Naina, wake up," a persistent voice says to me, but I am too asleep to realise the import of his words.

"Naina, you have to wake up sometime," the voice continues and I irritably swat the hand away that is shaking my shoulder.

"Sleep," I mumble. "Lem'me sleep."

I think the voice chuckles but I am too sleepy to care. Just then I feel something move and as I open my eyelids a couple of inches, the ground shifts.

"Aditya?" I squint as memories come rushing back.

"Yep."

I try to sit up and then realise that I am in his arms and he is taking me somewhere.

"What are you doing? Put me down," I say, slapping the hands which are holding me. "I said, *put me down!*"

"Whoa, lady, I was just putting you to bed."

"What happened?" I ask as soon as he places me down on the floor.

Shriya Garg

"The movie ended."

"Crap," I say. "What is the time?"

"One thirty a.m."

I sit down on the bed, "Wonderful. I am never going to hear the end of this."

"No worries, there are no parents at your place."

"You've forgotten Manya. I am surprised she hasn't called up to check whether I have been murdered already. You told her one hour. It has been nearly five."

"She called. I told her you were asleep."

"And she believed you?" I ask, raising my eyebrows. "She did not say that she knew you were kidding and I was probably lying in a ditch somewhere without my head?"

"She trusts me."

"Yeah, that was obvious because she waited for three hours before dialling. She must *really* trust you."

I massage my eyes, "I just want to sleep for a couple of more days."

"I guess Vandana hampered your last night's sleep."

"You guessed right."

I yawn.

"You can bunk here."

"No," I say and get up. "I am going home."

"*I* am taking you home. In *my* car," he reminds me.

"But what about my car?"

"Grab a metro to my place and take it tomorrow morning on your way to work."

"Fine, let me look for my crowbar and purse and then we'll go."

"The crowbar I don't know, but the purse is on the couch."

I go into the living room and the sight that greets me is quite surprising. Since the air-conditioning has been on, the room

Take One More Chance

is quite chilly and on the couch lies a thin blanket which now looks as though a herd of cows have passed over it. The table in front of it is laden with empty boxes of Chinese food and a stack of CDs. The scene seems quite cozy and all in all, not what I had in mind when I'd stomped over to kill him for dumping my best friend.

Which reminds me, Vandana never told me that she had been the one who had brought up the topic of 'parting ways'. If she wasn't upset about the break-up, then why did she let me come here to shout at Aditya?

I make a mental note to ask her as soon as morning dawns and grab my purse and crowbar to go and meet him at the door. Somehow I make it to the BMW in the parking, stumbling only a couple of times until he takes my hand. Talk about being awkward. The journey back home is made in comfortable silence except for the radio, which is still on.

"Thanks for the ride," I say as soon as we reach my house. I don't wait for him to come to open the door on my side and make it to the front steps.

"I would ask you for coffee," I turn to him and say after ringing the bell, "but I am really sleepy and if I made coffee, it would most likely contain salt and pepper."

He grins, "I wouldn't come in anyway. Got an early morning tomorrow."

"I am so sorry for staying this late."

"Hey, it is alright. I had fun."

"Me, too," I say, surprised to realise that it was true.

"Your last sentence would have felt good if you hadn't acted so surprised."

The door opens and Ria begins her diatribe even before the door is fully open. "So, Madam has finally decided to – oh, hi, Aditya."

Shriya Garg

"Hi, Ria, I am sorry to keep her so late. We just lost all track of time."

"Oh, it is perfectly understandable," she says in a heavy voice. "It is just us." She tries to shrug but has too much of adrenalin in her that the shrug turns into an awkward twist of shoulders.

"Thanks," Aditya replies in a voice absolutely dripping with honey. "Good-night, then," he says, turning to me.

"Whatever," I say, pushing through Ria and slamming the door of my bedroom behind me.

Naina Kashyap's Potential Suitor, Victim #5
By Vandana Sinha

Name: Aditya Khanna.

Age: 29.

Occupation: At some managerial post in Adobe, New Delhi

Place of Ambush: Undecided.

Height: 6'1".

Weight: 80 kg.

Physical Appearance: Tall, black haired and positively God-like. Has beautiful brown eyes, that are the colour of sparkling wine, has refined taste in clothing which he wears nicely because he is one of the very few men who are comfortable in their skin. Looks adorable in both Armani and Gap jeans. Beautiful hands with long, tapered fingers which are neither manicured nor calloused, because he uses his brain at work and not his hands. His sedentary lifestyle doesn't mean that he doesn't have a hot body either…Oh, I think that is it.

Uniform: Under construction at…

Naina: Vandana, what are you doing? (Vandana tries to hide the list but she snatches it from her hands.) What? Aditya? Are you frikkin crazy?"

Vandana: But, but, but…

OPERATION TERMINATED.

Naina Kashyap's Potential Suitor, Victim #6
By Naina Kashyap and Vandana Sinha (with inputs from Shaurya Kashyap)

Name: Nakul Mallya (and no, he is not related to the Mallyas).

Age: 26.

Occupation: Criminal lawyer.

Place of Ambush: District Park, Sector 9, Rohini.

Height: 5'9".

Weight: 70 kg.

Physical Appearance: Quite tall, black-haired and very light brown eyes.

Uniform: White T-shirt and shorts.

Attractive Features: Sharp, cutting to the point and can think on his feet. A great criminal lawyer.

Unattractive Feature(s): Loves pets way too much and is a health freak.

Interests: Dogs, cats and the concept of healthy living.

Atmosphere: Morning sunlight and sweaty joggers.

Beware: Don't ask him about his pets.

His Ideal Woman: A young woman who loves children – both human and animals. She should not object if he adopts more than just a couple stray dogs and cats and she should also understand that the secret to stay young is to live honestly, eat slowly and *not* lie about one's age.

Oh I love Sundays, I think as my eyes blink open. I am just turning to look at my clock when my phone rings.

What the – I mouth and then the caller's name registers.

"Holy shit!" I say as I throw back the sheets and look for my jogging clothes.

"Hey," I say quickly to Vandana, "I am awake; about to leave for the mission in ten minutes. Meet you in an hour at that roadside café finalised earlier. Over."

Quickly donning my jogging shoes, I rush out of the house and drive over to the park where we had decided to meet.

The park is full of early joggers from all walks of life – from old uncles with canes to old aunties in sneakers, determined to lose weight. I wasn't even aware that people actually got up at such an ungodly hour willingly.

I shake my head at their logic and look around for my maybe-husband. I find him crouched beside the ugliest dog I have ever seen. He seems to be a cross between a pug and a Dalmatian. I mean the dog, not Nakul. Nakul seems to be alright too, pretty unimpressive for a big-time criminal lawyer.

As I approach them, I realise that one of Nakul's hands is in the dog's mouth. I love animals, no offence, but I find that they create a lot of mess. I've never had a pet because my father always said that four animals were more than enough in one house. So, the concept of being really emotionally attached to a dog has always confused me a little. I think dogs are cute, but only from a distance. One stray dog had once tugged at my little blue skirt in kindergarten and chased me across one whole block. I have been wary of them ever since.

The dog notices me first and his sly black eyes focus on me as a hawk focuses on its prey.

I don't like you, buddy, I think.

No worries, I don't like you either, his eyes reply.

"Uh, hi," I say to the crouched Nakul and his head comes up. "I am Naina."

He gets up and holds out the hand which had been earlier in contact with the dog's saliva.

"Hi, I am Nakul."

"Yeah, I know – sorry, your hand," I say uneasily, motioning to the dog, "It was just in his mouth."

He laughs and holds out his other hand. I shake that.

"Meet Mickey," he says, patting the ugly Dalmatian/Pug. "I brought it only yesterday from the animal shelter, so we're just getting to know each other."

He pauses, as if waiting for me to greet the dog.

"Hi, Mickey," I finally say.

"You don't like dogs?" He picks up my hesitation.

"I do, except that I am a little afraid of them."

"Afraid of Mickey?" he gives a rumbling laugh and picks Mickey up, who doesn't look very light or like he appreciates being treated such.

"Mickey darling, say hello to Naina," Nakul cooes. Mickey Darling lifts one lip and snarls in reply.

"I think he senses your fear," Nakul says, frowning. "Animals sense such things."

I nod and he tries again, "Come on, Mickey, be nice. Say hello to the pretty girl standing in front of you."

He tries to take one of his fore paws but Mickey growls louder at his master. Nakul puts him down.

"I cannot understand. He likes everybody."

I kind of doubt that fact but I let it go.

"Well, then, let us walk," he says and picks up the dog's leash. "Do you often come here?"

"In the park? Usually in the evenings," I answer. "I am not much of an early-riser."

His mouth flattens in obvious disapproval but he doesn't comment. "I don't think there is a better perfume in the world than the early morning air," he says instead and closes his eyes and sniffs the air.

I disagree. Aditya's neck after a shower smelled a lot better.

"Yes, of course," I blurt out, guilty at the direction my thoughts have taken.

"So, Naina, tell me more about yourself. Your brother told me that you are an accountant."

"Yes."

"Has he told you anything about me?"

That you're a wily bastard.

"He said that you're very good at what you do."

He smiles a little, "I guess people could say that, but I have never thought of myself as a very successful lawyer. There are still so many criminals that go unpunished. How can I take credit for those who don't?"

"Oh," I say.

"Do you know why I always wanted to become a lawyer?"

I shake my head and he proceeds to tell me how his father was a lawyer, then his father and then *his* father.

"Not only it has been a family tradition, it is what I was born to do. When I stand in the courtroom with the man who had been raping his sixteen-year-old daughter for four years and finally made her pregnant, sitting in front of me, I feel so sick that I could do anything to see that man get the punishment he deserves. Some people are against hanging. I say that hanging for a man like him is too good."

I try not to grimace at what he is saying and notice the bright light of passion in his eyes. No wonder he is good at his job. He genuinely feels for those people.

"Oh, look at me rambling," he says with a sheepish grin. "I must have scared you with such heavy opening topics. So, Naina, your name is very beautiful – just like your eyes. I don't think I have seen that particular shade of brown anywhere."

"Not only in your work, you're very good in flattery as well."

He chuckles a little, "Me? A flatterer? *Au contraire*, darling, I have always believed that flattery is over-rated. I only give credit where it is due."

"Then I thank you for the compliment. And for the record, it was my mother's choice. When I was born, I could hardly open my eyes. She thought it fitting."

"I think so too. Tell me about your interests. What do you like to do in your spare time?"

"I like to read and write books."

"Oh really?" he appears surprised. "What sort of books do you read?"

"All sorts. I find John Grisham's courtroom novels very interesting."

"Those?" he scoffs. "I guess for a normal layman it would be very interesting. But reality is a little different from that."

"Have you read Sidney Sheldon's *Rage of Angels*?"

"I am afraid not."

"That is a spectacular novel. You would definitely find it interesting."

"I doubt it."

I frown, "Why?"

"I believe fiction to be rather exaggerated. I prefer non-fiction. Tell me about what you write."

"Oh, this and that," I say uneasily. I am interrupted by Mickey. He must have got tired of sniffing all the flowers because he bushes around him and turns to me.

"Ow," I say as he pokes his nose into my knee, "Please keep him away." I try to shrink but his nose doesn't go away.

"No, Mickey, no," Nakul says, tugging on his leash. Still the dog doesn't move. Meanwhile, his nose starts travelling upwards.

"No, M-Mickey," I stammer. "Bad place, b-b-bad place."

"Mickey," Nakul raises his voice a little. "Mickey, no... Mickey, bad dog. Mickey!"

No effect.

"I am sorry, Naina," Nakul says, tugging harder. "I don't know what has got into him." He moves the dog's jaw from the zipper of my shorts with his hands. The dog growls.

"Bad dog," Nakul scolds him. "What has happened to you?"

As sudden as it had come, the dog's interest in the female anatomy—mine—goes away. He removes his face from the centre of my shorts and gives a little whine.

"Mickey," Nakul is obviously concerned, "is there anything wrong? Do you want to pee?"

His head comes up at the last word and he seems even more agitated.

"I think that is it," Nakul says decisively. "Come on, crouch, Mickey, crouch." Mickey doesn't crouch and instead runs in a circle around Nakul.

Nakul bends down and pats the dog's back. "I am sorry, Naina, but I think something is wrong with him. I might have to take him to a vet."

My attention wanders to the dog, who is at that very moment, raising one of his hind legs. I watch the scene unfold in silent horror but am unable to do anything.

The dog pisses on Nakul's hand.

"What the *fuck?*"

And if that is not enough, a little of the dog's pee also lands on his shorts.

Watching Nakul's anger and annoyance over the naughty dog and seeing his white shorts stained yellow and brown gives me feel an absurd urge to giggle.

"What?" Nakul whirls towards me. "Are you *laughing* at me?"

"No, no," I say, covering my mouth with my hand. "Of, of course not. This is n-not at all f-funny."

"Damn right. Stupid asshole," he gets up and glares at the dog. "I save your life and you piss at me? You rascal."

He really is furious, I think.

"I could almost kick you," he spits at the dog. "Come on, Naina, let us get out of this park. I need to wash up."

I obediently follow and wonder idly that even this meeting with my potential suitor has been destroyed. It is almost as though fate is conspiring against me.

My mind begins working in over drive.

List #3: Naina Kashyap's Disastrous Dates

1) Victim #1: Ritesh Garg – I asked him if he was wearing any underwear – such a normal question for a to-be wife to ask. What does he do? Choke on his food and ends up in the hospital.

2) Victim #2: Nitin Sean – First he embarrassed me by singing a God-awful song in front of at least 30 people and then managed to place his fingers exactly where they would be slammed by my car's door. Not really my fault that he landed up in the hospital.

3) Victim #3: Rishab Bisht – Managed to drown all six feet of himself in a five-feet deep pool, and then coming out,

breaks his ankle. Again not my fault that he had to go to the hospital.

4) Victim #4: Nakul Mallya – He brought an awful dog of mysterious origin and then got angry when Mickey peed on him. I think the dog was taking revenge for being named Mickey. Wasn't Mickey a mouse, actually?

Well, at least he didn't land up in the hospital. As soon as the thought enters my mind, I freeze. Shit, I shouldn't have thought that.

God, Naina, why are you so *stupid*? I think of myself. Don't you know that you're cursed?

Now that I have said that Nakul hasn't ended up in the hospital, of course he had to. So when we are out on the main road and Nakul has washed himself as best as he could at a road-side tap, I just wait for it to happen.

"This meeting was definitely eventful," Nakul says, recovering some of his composure back. "I am so sorry it went this way."

Not your fault; it is me.

"It is okay," I say absently as I look around for any potential danger. Some early office-goers are headed our way as Nakul drops me to the café where I am to meet Vandana. Getting run over by a car? No, that doesn't sound likely. My dates die slow deaths. A car accident would be too quick.

"Listen, Naina, do you want to meet again?" Nakul asks and I think, *just wait until you're back home; or the hospital, actually.*

"Yes, I would love to," I say, craning my neck for any accidents waiting to happen.

Nakul grabs my arm, "Hey, stay on the footpath. You'll get run over otherwise."

Not me, but you, buddy.

Shriya Garg

I am only partially hearing what he is saying when I see a group of cyclists headed our way.

That is it.

Nakul partially turns towards me and doesn't notice what is approaching. The dog is walking behind us, so even he doesn't bark. The cyclists, a group of teenagers, are looking at a girl on the opposite sidewalk and sniggering rather than paying attention to the road.

"Nakul, move," I shout in a panic-stricken voice. I try to push him and myself out of harm's way but he is too heavy.

"What?"

"Nakul, the cyclists!" I scream but he is too slow. As soon as I had taken a couple of steps towards the left along with the ungrateful dog, six cyclists crash into Nakul in a line – one after the other.

Smack!

"Hey, watch…"

Smack, smack!

"Ouch, please…"

Smack, smack, smack!

He falls on the road and nearly disappears because three cycles along with their riders have covered him completely. There is nothing of him except a lot of groaning noises.

The other cyclists brake too late.

Smack, smack, smack, smack!

A policeman on duty at the red light next to us comes over. 'Hey, boys, don't you watch where you're going? Now, who have you run over?"

And…goal! Naina Kashyap has done it again.

Victim #4 en route to the hospital.

7:30 a.m.

"He sounds like a nice guy," Vandana says after she has finished listening – and laughing – at the whole thing. "Maybe you should have gone with him to the hospital – held his hand through the ordeal and all that."

"Yuck," I make a face. "His hand was covered in dog-piss."

"Oh, yeah, I forgot. You want another coffee?"

"Nope. I have already had enough adrenalin for the day."

She pats my hand sympathetically, "It happens, sweetie. Don't be disheartened."

"Are you serious? Give me one example of this happening to somebody else? You know what, Vandana? I think I am cursed."

"Don't be absurd!" her eyes light up. "But now that you mention it, I think there are signs."

"Signs? What signs?"

"God is telling you that these men are not for you. That your prince is just waiting around the corner but you have to first kiss all those toads to get to him."

"How many toads have you kissed?" I ask angrily at her dreamy look.

"Hundreds."

"I haven't even kissed a couple of them. I don't think I can do this any more."

"Oh, honey, don't give up now."

"Aditya was right," I say in abject misery. "I really should come with a warning sign."

"Aditya is crazy. He also said that you are the most interesting woman he has ever met. Don't take him seriously."

He really said that? You never told me.

I clear my throat because I cannot clear my *brain*. "But I feel so guilty for injuring all those nice guys."

"Hey, you didn't injure them. God did. And if it is His will, then who can question it?"

I stop stirring my coffee. "What has happened to you?"

"Oh, this God thing? It is because of the new guy I am going out with. Vedaant. He is into religion."

"Tell me about him," I say as I begin eating my sandwich.

"He is really cute. Not great in the looks department, but cute. And he brings me flowers every time we meet. Kisses great; nice body but is quite dumb. No, I mean *really* dumb. And not in a good way. Let us see how it goes."

"You're certainly quick. I don't understand how I ever thought that you were shy. So, where did you two meet?"

"At a mall. Both of us wanted the same CD, but the store had only one in stock. He said, 'Go ahead, buy it,' and I replied, 'No, you buy it.' This continued for a couple of minutes until the bemused clerk said, 'You can have it for free if it means that you'd allow the next customer to pay.'"

"Cute."

"Yeah. We shared a pizza, then watched a movie as well. Exchanged numbers and finally came back home."

"I wish I had a decent date like that."

"At least Aditya wasn't there this time to mock you."

Which actually took all the fun out of it. I must have become used to him taking the poor men to the hospital. Thank God for the traffic policeman this time.

Of course, that was the only reason I missed Aditya. A little. Not much; just a little.

"Well, I have to rush if I have to reach work on time," I say, eyeing Vandana's pretty blue shirt and jeans with envy.

"Me, too. Hey, so do you want me to hunt for the next victim?"

"Um, no, please. Not for the time being. I am done with kissing toads. I want the prince now."

"You'll get him," Vandana predicts confidently as I pay for the breakfast.

"I know. I just hope that I get him before it is midnight and the carriage turns back into the pumpkin."

"Hi, guys," I say to my class. "How are you all?"

"Hello, *didi*," they chorus. "We are well, thank you. And how are you?"

I smile at their confident answer and say, "Pretty awful. But that is for later. Oh, hello, little ones, who are you two?"

There is an addition to the batch – two little twin girls.

"*Main Sudha hoon, aur yeh meri chhoti behen, Malla.*" one of them says in Hindi. (I am Sudha and this is my younger sister, Malla.)

I try not to frown. These two little girls obviously know no English and can't mix with the rest of the batch. I hate such moments when I have to turn down new additions. There is such light of hope in those eyes which would have to get crushed.

"Sweethearts, have you ever gone to school?"

"*Ji,* madam, *hum doosri tak gaye the.*" (Yes, madam, we'd gone to school till the second grade.)

I think over it. I just can't turn them down. Of late, new children are coming more often. Maybe I could take one more class, or ask somebody else to do it. Any of my friends could take it up readily. The only problem is that nobody knows about this. It isn't because I am ashamed of this – God knows I am not – but because it feels too personal to share with anybody. But I can't afford to be selfish now.

"Listen, darlings," I bend down and tell them the whole plan. They have to look for more willing students and then meet me here again in a couple of days.

They smile at me and Malla, the younger one who hasn't said anything till now, bends down to touch my feet.

"Hey, hey, hey," I say, picking up the little girl who is way too thin for a 13-year old. "No touching feet, please. Just go home now and oh, don't worry about books and pencils. I have extra."

They happily go home and I return my attention to the others. We do some revision and then discuss the Commonwealth Games, which had begun in New Delhi then. We then proceed to division and multiplication. In the end come the thought for the week, which is one by Bertrand Russell: "The whole problem with the world is that fools and fanatics are always so certain of themselves, but wiser people so full of doubts."

We take a while to understand its meaning, but Laxmi, as always, grasps it quicker than anybody else and explains it to the whole class. She is one exception to the quote I think and that familiar sadness overtakes me.

But this time I know what to do. Come high hell or water, Laxmi is going to go to school. There is enough injustice in the world without the poor girl suffering in some woman's kitchen and doing the dishes.

I don't know why I hadn't thought of that before. Maybe it is that little girl touching my feet, which makes me realise I am not all that helpless, or maybe it is just the helplessness of the past few months of watching all my attempts at a happy married life and secure future go down the drain.

"Laxmi, I need to talk to you," I say after the class has wrapped up and everybody is ready to go.

She grows nervous at my tone but I give her a reassuring smile, "By what time do you have to be home, sweetie?"

"In one hour."

"Good. Let us have something to eat then."

As soon as the words are out of my mouth, I notice the other kids' reaction. They try to hide their hurt faces but I am too ashamed of myself to notice that. Burgers for six people at McDonalds? Not more than two hundred bucks, and yet, here I am.

"Guys, let us all have something to eat. Is there anybody who has to be home early today?"

Suman raises her hand, obviously disappointed, but I say, "Then we'll get something packed for you. Come on, I am hungry."

Everybody smiles at that, the hurt look vanishing and I thank God that children can forgive elders so easily even when we are not worthy of it. How easier it would have been for everybody if the adults could learn that?

So, we go to McDonalds where I tell all the children to look at the display boards and order anything they want. The children do so happily and the handsome guy behind the counter smiles at me with a glint in his eyes as he sees the obviously out-of-place children having the time of their lives. At a McDonald's, for Christ's sake.

Some people eye us with raised brows as they see the kids create a ruckus, but usually everybody at that place has a smile for the kids. The world is not such a bad place to live in actually.

We have burgers, Cokes and ice-creams and laughter. It is about an hour-and-a-half when everybody is ready to leave. Our table is more littered than the others but even then, the same guy behind the counter winks at me as he tells the cleaning guy to mop it up.

I smile back at him and he hesitates, but comes over. I tell everybody to wipe their faces with the paper napkin and say 'Hi' to the guy.

"I am Vishal," he says, stretching out his hand,

"I am Naina," I say and shake his hand.

He holds out the money I'd paid for the food. "Please, let this be my treat."

I am shocked, "Oh, no, I really can't accept this from…"

"I am not poor," Vishal says. "I am helping out a friend, actually. I am a civil engineer on my better days."

"Oh, no! Still, I can't."

"Please, we all should do what we can to help. I feel ashamed of myself."

"Then do something more productive," I say on an impulse. "I need someone to teach another batch of such kids once a week for two hours. Can you do that?"

He is obviously taken aback and I almost bite my tongue. The guy just wants to spend five hundred bucks when he earns thousands every month. Why would he tutor them when he can watch from outside?

But he surprises me some more with his smile, "I'd love to. Tell me the place and time."

I smile back and tell him. He promises to meet me two days later and we shake hands again.

As soon as we are out of the restaurant, I turn to Laxmi, "I still need to talk to you, honey."

So, after everybody has gone back home, we sit in my car and I begin talking.

"Laxmi, I want you to go to school."

She gives a startled squeal of delight before reality dawns, "But no, it is not possible."

I give her a determined smile, "Laxmi, how much do you earn in a month?"

"Six hundred rupees."

"I'll pay your parents six hundred rupees a month. But then, they can't make you work anywhere. I mean it, Laxmi. You must go to school and after that do your homework."

Her black little eyes stare at me and there is only resignation there. The child is scared to *dream*.

I start the engine. "Let us go to your home. I've had enough of this stupidity."

Two hours later, I come out of her little shanty – tired, but happy. There had been a roaring fight, a lot of pot-banging and cursing but in the end, they'd come around. Laxmi is going to join a private school. She'd have to start with the second grade, of course, but she is bright and I am sure she would catch up quickly. Her Maths is already better than a second-grader's. She may have to work a little harder than the rest of her classmates, but she can do it. Happily.

Laxmi was crying by the time I'd left her. She said that she prayed for me every night before going to sleep. And because the little girl had looked so sad, I told her to pray that I'd find a good husband, at which she'd laughed.

I go home and tell my Dad about it. He looks grim.

"You can't fix everything in this world, Naina," he says.

"Dad, I am not trying to fix everything in this world. She is just a little girl. And she has huge potential, Dad. You just meet her once, and you'd have no qualms about what I am doing."

"It is a good thing you're doing, Naina, but education is not cheap."

At that, I sigh and get into my accountant mode. "Dad, I earn a freaking ninety thousand a month. Since I live with you, I have no rent to pay and no water or electricity bills either. So, my only expenditure is on the maintenance of my car and shopping for clothes and books. Ten thousand rupees here and there, at the maximum. That means, every month, around eighty thousand rupees go to the bank. If I calculate correctly, Laxmi's fees, books, uniform and bus fee would cost me about five thousand a month. Can't I do that much? Not even a month's salary for the whole year."

"You're a good girl, Naina," my Dad says and kisses my forehead, "and you make me very proud. But think about this:

you are married and you have your own children's fee to pay. Then you'd have to pay your own electricity and water bills, though of course, you'd have your husband's added support. Do you think he would like these extra-curricular activities of yours?"

"I wouldn't ever marry a man who would not like what I am doing." Then suddenly an idea occurs to me, "Dad, Laxmi's father beats her. I know what I will do. I have a plan."

"I know that look. What?"

"As soon as I'm married, I am going to adopt her."

"Honey, don't be insane. Listen to yourself! There are lots of other ways you can help."

"Please don't patronise me," I say with quiet determination.

"Then stop acting that way."

"Why is it stupid? Preity Zinta adopted 34 orphans on her thirty-fourth birthday. Shilpa Shetty promised to donate 6,000 rupees to charity for every six her IPL team hit the previous season. You don't think they are stupid."

My father's lips form a straight line. "You are comparing yourself to Preity Zinta and Shilpa Shetty. They make *millions* every year and Preity is unmarried. Due to their popularity, they get certain immunity from society. What would people say if *you* adopted a 12-year old child as soon as you get back from your honeymoon? Children are a lifetime commitment and sometimes even with your very own child, you have rows and you slap them. Wouldn't you then be doing the same to Laxmi what she has been accepting in the past?" he asks, his voice rising. "It is not always fun and games and laughter. What would your husband think when he wants you to have another child – *his* child? What would your in-laws say? Would they treat Laxmi and your other child equally?"

The enormousness of the task begins to scare me, but I lift up my chin and even though I am shaking with repressed rage inside, I try not to show it.

Shriya Garg

"Dad, I think I know a little about those children and about Laxmi since I have been teaching them for the past one year. You didn't know about it, but I have been giving her and six other children private tuitions once a week because their parents are too poor to afford school, or even let their child spend eight hours daily in schoolwork. They need the money which their children make. After seeing them beam at me when they can draw a straight line using a pencil and scale, I become aware that parenting is not just *fun* and *games* and *laughter*. Sometimes the burden of all their hopes makes me so sad that I almost can't bear it. They believe that I can perform miracles; that McDonalds is an unheard luxury and that Luxor pens are the stuff of their dreams. They haven't grown up watching Tom and Jerry and Tweety. They have never had the chance to complain of long socks or demanded shorter skirts for school. They never even got a chance to celebrate the first day of the summer break. I know you won't understand it, but please, believe me, they are more mature than any of us in this room. If Laxmi knows that I am going to scold her for a good reason, she would accept it as her due."

I take a shaky breath and continue, "Nobody can *not* love Laxmi after meeting her. And I would love Laxmi enough so that she never feels that it is lacking from any other side. There is no problem with Laxmi. She is not some kind of *diseased pet*, for God's sake, that what the neighbourhood will *talk*. What is the guarantee that the baby I'd give birth to wouldn't be crippled, blind, deaf or even *dead*? Mothers have taken care of their children even when the child has had more serious problems than not being able to read above the third-grade level!"

Till an hour, the idea of adopting Laxmi hadn't even occurred to me. Now I was sure that come high heaven or hell, I was going to get a daughter.

"I don't know why I bother to argue with you," my father says resignedly. "When have you ever listened to what I have said, anyway? This is between you and your future spouse, whoever the poor chap may be."

"Fine," I say in a huff.

"You can go back to your room now."

"Thank you, Your Majesty."

I am sitting in my cabin, happily contemplating my last meeting with Laxmi and Vishal when there is a knock on the door.

Before I can answer, the door swings open.

"Hello, Naina."

I get up, "Good morning, sir. What can I do for you?"

To say that Mr Abhijeet Mukherjee is an unimpressive person would be a hell of an overstatement. He is a wily, oily-haired man and how he has reached the managerial position is anybody's guess. He wears custom-tailored suits which are usually covered with fishy fingerprints. All the women in the department scurry away at the sight of him because he has a very annoying habit of looking at one's bust-line while talking to them – sorry, *us*.

He has made passes at everyone from his secretary to the cleaning *bai*, i.e. except me. I could never tell whether to be relieved or annoyed.

"Naina," his gaze drops to my mouth and travels lower, "Some friends of the boss are coming from London for a meeting with him and he wants us to entertain them for one night. So I've organised a small party on Halloween for them at a farmhouse."

I nod, confused.

"I know that we always don't see eye to eye on everything, but I would like you to be present with me to entertain them."

"I am sorry, sir, but I don't get you."

"I want you to be the hostess for the evening."

WHAT? WHY? Why me?

"Yes, sir, of course."

"Good, I knew I could count on you. Get the address of the farmhouse from my secretary and also the telephone numbers of the guests. It is going to be a masquerade and I want you to send over some masks for those ten people to choose from."

"Yes, sir."

He nods and leaves the room. I drop down on my seat as Sanjana, a colleague, sees the boss leaving and enters.

"What was Fishman doing over here?"

"Some masquerade on Halloween for some guests from London."

"Yeah, I know about that. The whole office is invited," she pauses delicately. "Rumour is that you are going to be the hostess of the evening."

Sanjana is a nice, bright girl and I usually like her but right then, I couldn't help throwing her a dirty look, "Gossip mill is right."

"What?" she whoops with laughter. "Thank God I'd be there for moral support. Just imagine the time you're going to have, dodging his hands under the table."

"Get lost."

She laughs and turns to leave as I turn my eyes to the desktop in front of me.

"See ya," she grins. "Wouldn't wanna be ya."

"How do I look?" I ask Sanjana as we stand at the entrance of the farmhouse, with bouquets and drinks, waiting for the guests to arrive.

She checks out my long, white gown, which trails the floor and hugs my curves. I had fluffed my hair and was wearing small diamond studs. I looked good and I knew it.

"You look like a medieval princess. Where did you find this gown anyway?"

"Vandana Escort Service," I reply. "She took me to places that I didn't know even existed in Delhi."

"And how do I look?"

I check her out. She is wearing a lacey green gown. "Horrifying."

She smiles, "The spirit of Halloween. This colour is definitely scary. When Fishman announced that there was going to be a Halloween party, I wanted to be Count Dracula, but then I got to know about the no-costume thing."

"It is dumb, I know. Halloween and no dressing up. But they find Asians already scary, and Fishman didn't want to scare them even more."

"Idiots," Sanjana says with a snort.

"I know. Oh, here they come."

Three Mercedes pull up at the kerb and the chauffeur opens the door of the Mercedes in the front. The boss arrives just in time.

"Give me the bouquet," he whispers to me, pasting on a fake smile and walking forward to greet them.

"Hello, sir, such a pleasure…Just this way, sir. Sanjana, show them the way…We hope you have had a pleasant stay in New Delhi…Yes, I am sure, sir, that you are going to enjoy this party…" Blah blah.

I follow his footsteps and add a couple of comments. Finally, when all of them have been greeted and we move inside to bad music and worse food. Fake carved pumpkins and spider-webs are arranged around the room and there is an open bar, so things seem to be alright.

It isn't until an hour later when other guests – the boss's other associates and friends – begin turning up that I know things are going to go down. Way down.

"What the hell is *he* doing here?"

"Who are you talking about?" Sanjana asks, half her face covered by a green-feathered mask, mirroring my white-feathered one.

I point to Aditya Khanna, who is walking into the room at that very moment. He is dressed in a starched white shirt and a knee-length black waist-coat with an honest-to-god cravat. He looks like the rakish duke of every historical romance novel ever written and the effect he casts upon the room is just as identical.

"Sweet baby Jesus," Sanjana breathes next to me and then gushes, "do you know him? Is he single? *Can I have him?*"

Have I ever mentioned that she has a very annoying habit of salivating over any decent-looking guy who glances her way and great-looking guys who don't glance her way?

"Yep, I know him," I answer. "Yes, he is single. And yes, you can have him."

Then as if he could somehow hear my voice across fifty people, he turns his head from the woman he's been talking to and glances in my direction. He spots me and smiles from ear to ear.

"Introduce me," Sanjana hisses in my ear. "*Now.*"

"Yeah, whatever," I say and make my way towards Aditya through the throng of guests.

"Hi!" he says, meeting me mid-way.

"Hi!" Is it the heat that is making my voice so husky?

We stand there awkwardly for a while because shaking hands seems too formal and hugging seems too snug, so we do neither. Beside me, Sanjana coughs.

"Oh, yeah, um, Aditya, this is Sanjana, my friend. Sanjana, this is Aditya, my-um…" I pause because I can not find the right word to use for him.

"Mortal enemy sounds too juvenille?" Aditya asks with a smile.

"Uh, yeah. Sanjana, this is the man who has been put on earth for the sole purpose of making my life miserable."

"The pleasure is all mine," he grins in reply as Sanjana and Aditya shake hands.

"So, what are you doing here?" he asks me.

"These are the boss's friends. We were just asked to entertain them. You?"

"My boss also got an invite. He couldn't come because he had to take his wife to dinner today. It is his twenty-fifth anniversary. He sent me instead with his secretary."

"Secretary? Which secretary?"

Like my words have conjured her, an enormous woman draped in a sari, that looked like it had been pasted with as many stones as the craftsman could find, sidles up next to him.

"Aditya," the woman who looks to be at least fifty years young pouts – no, I am not even kidding – and adds in broken English, "Why don't you introduce me to your girlfriends?"

"Saroj," Aditya says a trifle uneasily and removes her paunchy hand from his forearm, "these are not my girlfriends."

"Oho *ji*, they are girls, and they are your friends. Who else is a girlfriend?" she replies and places her hand exactly at the place from which it had been removed a second ago.

"Uh, I don't know. You are right," he says and shifts his weight from foot to foot. I can not help chuckling. He glares at me and then takes my hand.

"Naina was just about to introduce me to her friend. Weren't you, chumkins?"

Chumkins?

He looks down at me with an intimate smile while I am sure my face contains nothing but shock. He squeezes my hand and grits his teeth at my blank face.

"Uh-huh-yeah…"

Saroj's thick hands come between us as she tries to make some space for herself. "I meet him, too."

Aditya sighs in resignation and drops my hand.

"Show us the way," he gestures.

I lead him to Fishman, who tries the same tricks with me that Saroj had just tried with Aditya.

"Give my best wishes to your boss," Fishman says, placing a hand on my waist. I move slightly forward so that I am not in contact with him any more but it doesn't take him long to regain the lost ground.

"Yes, Mr Mukherjee, definitely," Aditya replies and makes small talk. "And I must add that the party is really great."

A waiter passes us, carrying glasses of champagne, and even though I strictly stay away from alcohol – my father would kill me if he ever got to know – I pick one up.

A couple of minutes later, the dancing starts. Fishman leads me to the floor. Even though our faces are covered with masks, I can still feel his dirty gaze roving over my modest décolletage. He holds me closer than necessary and I push at his hands, emboldened by the alcohol I've consumed.

"Sir, please, if you'd behave."

"You are very bold, Naina," he says quietly instead. "A woman not afraid to speak her mind. Too bad God hasn't made more of your kind."

"Yeah, too bad," I say, barely paying him any attention.

Shriya Garg

"Tell me, Naina, do you think of us as friends?"

I am appalled, "No."

"Good," his hand caresses my arm and I am almost ready to throw up. "Friendship between the employer and employee is never a good thing. However..." his sentence trails off and thankfully, before I kill him, Aditya interrupts.

"If you don't mind – may I cut in?"

"Thank you, yes," I say before Fishman can say no.

"Nice boss you've got there," Aditya says in my ear as we sway lightly to the rhythm. And even though he is smiling, it is a tight smile and it does not reach his eyes, which look kind of hard to me.

"Are you pulling my leg?"

"No," he replies. "Do you want me to beat him up?"

"No, I need the job."

"I read your book," he says instead. "It is brilliant. What are your current plans?"

"I think I have finally reached the ending. I am busy writing the synopsis and query letters."

"Best of luck with them. I knew a couple of editors and publicists back in New York. If you want, I can ask them to have a look at it for you. They wouldn't think twice before doing it."

I know my eyes are shining when I look at him, "You'd do that?"

This time when he smiles, it is real.

"Sure. I would like to return the favour."

"What favour?" I breathe.

"The favour of not killing me. I have spent more time with you than all your dates combined and I am still walking on my two legs. You must *really* like me."

As soon as the light comes, it goes out again.

"So we are back to that."

"Yep," he grins. "I shouldn't have offered to beat up that guy. Another hour with you and that problem would have been taken care of."

"At least this time I can look forward to it."

The song ends and we move off the dance floor. We spot Saroj approaching and Aditya leads me promptly in the other direction. "I call her the Pit Bull. She has a son who is not much younger than me."

I smile, "She is cute."

"I could still hand you over to your boss."

He gives me a sideways smile. "I was just kidding," I amend.

We move around the room and I check with the caterer if everything is going alright. The tables are set and the liquor isn't in any danger of running out. Yep, everything is alright.

I see Sanjana glaring at me from the other side of the hall and wince.

"What happened?"

"Sanjana. She wanted to hook up with you."

"Who?"

"Sanjana," I hiss. "Remember the girl I introduced you to?"

"She is cute," he says, "but not my type."

"What is your type?" I ask.

He thinks about it for a second, "Well, come to think of it I don't have a type."

"But you're single and she is also single," I point out.

"Even you're single," he says in a reasonable tone. "That isn't any reason to hook up."

"You're right. I am doomed anyway."

He squeezes my hand, "It'll be okay. Tell me what you're doing these days."

We talk for a while as I play hostess, down some more alcohol and evade Fishman, Sanjana and Pit Bull.

Half an hour later, we settle down three tables away from each other for dinner.

On my left is Fishman and on my right is another guy from the finance department whose name I don't know. I silently chew my mushroom ravioli as Fishman makes conversation next to me.

Five minutes later, he turns to me, "Is everything going alright?"

"Yes," I reply, after I have swallowed my mushroom. "Everything is running smoothly."

He pats my hand, "I haven't thanked you properly for all you've done, Naina. I'd be sure to talk to the boss about a bonus..."

I feel like a hooker being paid for services rendered but force myself to take another bite.

Didn't he say that I was not afraid of speaking my mind? In that case, he was wrong because right now what I want to do is pull out my four-inch heels and smack him on the head with its pointed tip. But, instead, I smile weakly and remove my hand from beneath his.

"No, really," he says, seeing me withdraw my hand. "You have been a tremendous help. You'd be an asset to any organisation you work for and we're extremely glad that you chose us to be your employer."

Okay, you know how girls are always comparing the worst pick-up lines? At a recent list I'd come across on some website, the one at the top had been, 'Are you busy tonight at 3:00 a.m.?' and 'Your legs must be tired because you've been running through my mind all night.' Well, the one that my boss had used right now definitely topped the list. Tremendous asset to any employer? Yeah, I am definitely that, though not in the way he means.

"You know, Naina," he continues, oblivious to the ominous way I am using my fork to stab the poor mushroom in my plate, "earlier, I used to be a little wary of you. You have a hard edge to you, which is undoubtedly very sexy but just as scary. Fortunately for me, I have recently seen you losing that hard edge. It seems you are not as determined to scare away any guy who – God forbid – expresses any interest in you. You're like what I was in kindergarten. Do you know how I was in kindergarten?"

The kind who liked to play gynaecologist-gynaecologist *with young, unsuspecting and naïve female kindergarteners.*

"No. How?"

"I used to pull the hair of the girl I liked."

"How cute." Not.

He swallows my lie.

"I know, right?" When he sees that my hands are occupied with my fork and knife, he pats my knee and I nearly jump out of my chair.

"Miss, are you alright?" the guy sitting next to me asks and I almost answer in negative.

"Yes," I reply through tight lips and turn towards my boss. Now, a little verbal flirting is tolerable, but this is taking things too far. The only reason I've not thrown my drink at him is because, though his notoriety and infidelity are famous across all departments, he has never been known to have taken any unwilling partners. There must be something that women find attractive, because a case of rape or force has never been reported.

"Sir," I say, again taking out my anger on the food, "I am sorry but this type of conduct would not be acceptable by me."

"Oh, come on, Naina," Fishman laughs and waves his hand as though I have just cracked the joke of the year, "You and I – we can be frank with each other. We know what we want in life.

I don't want emotional baggage, and after seeing your love life…"

I am blindly stabbing whatever is in my plate mainly because I can't stab my boss without going to prison.

"…I am quite convinced that you're after the same thing…"

How dare he? How dare he? I think and stab the food harder so that bits of it fall out of the platter. A screeching voice arises as the metal of my fork comes in contact with the metal of the plate.

"Naina," a familiar voice says behind me and taps on my shoulder. "Can I talk to you for a second?"

Aditya Khanna has committed perhaps one of the biggest faux pas of the corporate world, but I am so glad to see him that I push back my chair and leave my boss in the middle of the sentence.

"*How dare he? How dare he?*" I screech. "I am going to report him the first thing in the morning for sexual harassment."

He doesn't reply and instead hands me a flute of champagne and takes one for himself. We both drink it in one gulp.

"No police officer is going to listen to you. Patting your knee and verbal innuendoes do not qualify as sexual harassment," he says and tosses back another drink.

"You're forgetting Manya," I say as I do the same to my second drink. "She is going to have his ass out of his leather chair and into a prison bed before he realises what hit him."

"I certainly hope so. Men like him are despicable."

I am so angry that I do not even agree with that statement but I am busy thinking of another more degrading word.

We occupy two raised chairs directly in front of the bar and order gin and tonic.

"Classic a-hole," I finally reply, watching Fishman eye another buxom blonde sitting in front of him.

"I have an idea," Aditya says and sits up. Both of us can feel the effect of the alcohol but our brains are too clouded for us to pay our slurred words much attention.

"Idea? What idea?"

"Let us teach Mukherjee a lesson."

"Fishman? What lesson?" I slur stupidly.

"Waiter," Aditya calls out loudly to a young man passing by us. "Waiter! Wait, that is not a waiter. Oops, sorry, mister," he roars with laughter. "Your clothes confused me. Black and white and that tie – sorry." We look at each other as the offended man throws us a contemptuous glance and leaves as we laugh.

"Waiter," Aditya tries again. "Yes, you. Tell me your name."

A young man standing in front of us patiently answers, "Raju."

"Raju, nice name. So, Raju, uh…" he turns to me, suddenly confused. "What was my idea? I forgot my idea."

I am confused as well. "You didn't tell me your idea."

He squints, "I didn't. Oh! I forgot –· this stupid gin – uh, yes! I remember it." He turns towards Raju who is still standing there patiently, obviously used to the whims of the rich.

"Yes, sir?"

"Raju, tell me, brother, how much do you earn in a day at this dumb farmhouse?"

"Five hundred rupees, sir."

"Nice salary," Aditya comments, sitting up straighter. "Never knew waiters earned so much. Naina, did you know this? Never mind. Raju, I am just a trifle bit dizzy. So, Raju, since this is most likely the last party for today, you would get your salary, won't you?"

"Yes, sir."

"So, I bet you wouldn't mind working a little extra for a bonus?"

The bartender who must have been just pretending not to listen, leans forward at this point, "No fights over here, mister."

"Fight? Me?" Aditya keeps an innocent hand over his heart. "No, we're just having a bit of fun here. No fights." In the spirit of the no-fight announcement, he places his arm around Raju and pulls him closer.

"See that guy over there?" he asks, pointing towards Fishman. Seeing his pointed hand, he puts it down and shakes his head as if to clear it. "Yes, that oily-haired one. And you see this pretty girl over here?" he points to me and then again puts his finger down. "Pointing is bad," he whispers to himself. "She is my brother's fiancée," he lies outrageously, even when he is half-drunk. "And that oily man is her boss. My brother has just left the building because he saw her boss patting her over here," he pats Raju's butt and I stifle a giggle.

"Now, my brother, despite being a very nice guy, is very paranoid. You know, paranoid, don't you, brother? I mean, he could never understand how he landed up with such a beautiful woman like her, and so is always suspicious."

Raju nods in understanding.

"And the boss is very bad. Very bad." Aditya opens his mouth wide to emphasise the 'very bad.' "He touches my future sister-in-law *there*. You know where, don't you? Yes, so he – the boss – touched her *there* and her fiancé *saw* it and now he thinks that both of them are having an affair and he left. See how upset she is. Naina, show her how upset you are," he orders and I obediently pull my mouth into a frown. And because I am feeling very funny sitting there like that, I decide to get into my role and stick out my lower lip. I even pretend to wipe invisible tears and hide my face in my hands.

Aditya kicks my leg with his foot to indicate I am over-acting and I immediately stop.

"Now, we were thinking, Raju brother, of teaching that slime a lesson."

Raju nods in compassion.

"What do you want me to do, brother?" Raju asks, both of them getting brotherly over my pitiful condition.

"I was thinking," Aditya says, taking another sip of his drink, "if somebody accidentally – *accidentally*, you know – spilled a boiling hot cup of coffee over the man's hair, what would happen?"

I laugh out aloud at the picture he has painted and then remember that I was not supposed to giggle.

"Something not very nice," Raju says.

"Don't you worry, Raju brother, I would compensate you well for the scolding you're going to get from your manager."

"I wouldn't need that compensation." Brave Raju shakes his hand as he observes the piece of filth sitting comfortably, finishing his cake. "It is the duty of us men to preserve the honour of women like your sister."

"Man, she is not my sister," Aditya says, immediately offended. "Sister-in-law, I said, and even that is not final."

Raju nods once more, and after taking another glance at the water-less sobs coming out of me, leaves to find a steaming hot cup of coffee.

Both of us settle back in our chairs to enjoy the show. We are not disappointed. Barely two minutes later Raju enters, carrying a whole tray, full of steaming coffee cups, and heads directly towards Fishman's table.

"Do you think he would get fired?" I ask Aditya, belatedly concerned about Raju.

"Nah. Accidents happen all the time."

144   *Shriya Garg*

I smile, appeased and again turn towards the show. It happens exactly as we'd planned. Raju carefully moves between the tables, expertly handling the tray in one hand raised above his head and just as he is behind Fishman, he strikes his foot against one of the legs of the chair and pretends to fall. The eight cups land on different parts of Fishman's suit and he roars like a dragon that has been challenged.

A cup clangs on the table and breaks, dividing its contents between the tablecloth and Fishman's lap. A couple of them land on the floor, splashing his trousers' legs in quite a wonderful pattern and the remaining four land on different areas of his hair and shoulders.

There is a huge commotion as Fishman calls poor Raju every bad name he can think of, complains about poor pathetic people who can't even hold a cup properly and questions his parentage and the status of his parents' marital status. Raju meanwhile stands silently with his head bowed as Fishman shouts at the manager, "Do you know who I am? Do *you*? I want this pathetic excuse for a server fired this instant, if you want to keep running your farmhouse."

"Oh shit," I whisper guiltily to Aditya.

In front of us, Raju is led outside the premises but as he passes us, he winks at me. Aditya swears.

"They're not going to fire him," he predicts confidently, his speech somewhat normal again as the adrenalin in our bodies has overcome the effect of the liquor.

"Are you sure?"

"Look at him, Naina. Raju wouldn't have agreed to it in the first place if he had even a shadow of doubt that he'd be fired. He cannot afford that luxury. I think he is probably going to be kept out of the main room for a couple of days and then things are going to return to normal."

I nod in agreement and because we have two drinks in front of us, we pick them up and toast to Raju.

"Cheers."

Pit Bull enters our field of view at that time.

"Oh no," Aditya says and ducks his head but it is useless because she has already spotted him and is moving towards us with all the determination of a bull who has been shown her red flag.

"Hello, Ms. Saroj," I say, trying to be extra nice because I am still feeling guilty for burning Fishman and getting rid of him. "Are you enjoying the party?"

"Yes *ji*, yes, party very pretty," she says, flopping down next to Aditya. "Aditya, where you gone and leaving me?"

"Ms. Saroj, I don't think I have introduced you to Naina, my girlfriend," Aditya says loudly.

"You have, *ji*, you have," she replies, thinning her lips as old aunties do in disapproval when they see a girl in tank top riding a bike with her boyfriend; which is actually ironic because in our past conversation, she was the one who had mentioned Sanjana and me as his girlfriends.

Aditya takes my hand from across the table. "We are going to be engaged next month, aren't we, sweetheart?"

"Yes," I reply and take another fortifying sip of my gin which mysteriously keeps refilling itself.

"How nice," Pit Bull says, her tone conveying exactly what she thinks of our dopily staring at each other. I can see that she is thinking that I am trying to be coquettish.

"So, what do you do, Miss Naina?"

And the inquisition begins. From the number of questions she asks about my hobbies and siblings and parents, I feel like I have asked her to be the President of United States instead of her beloved Aditya's wife. Come to think of it, technically, I hadn't even *asked* to be Aditya's wife.

Once she excuses herself to go to the loo and Aditya looks at me with a miserable expression on his face. She is, of course, going to come back.

"Aw, poor baby," I say. "I know what to do."

He puts aside his glass of liquor. Apparently, his level of grief even liquor cannot cure.

"What?"

"My turn, my turn," I say happily and even clap my hands once. "Hey, give me a break; I am drunk."

"What your turn?"

"Since you taught Fishman a lesson for me, I am going to return the favour."

Aditya sits up in alarm and orders a cup of coffee. "What? I don't want to burn the poor woman."

"I am not going to burn her, for God's sake."

"Then?"

"There is nothing wrong with her except a little obsession with you, which is perfectly understandable."

The coffee arrives and after offering it to me, he drinks it.

I stand up and my vision sways. I grab his arm for support and then smile brightly, "I met a man a couple of hours ago."

He tries to follow the conversation, "Two hours ago? What am I, then?"

I giggle, "No, silly, I am talking about an old man." I lower my voice as if we are plotting a conspiracy, "For *her*." I point towards the washrooms with my head.

I notice that he has not grasped a word of my brilliant idea and I drag him out of the chair.

"Mr Pandey," I beam at the seventy-five-year old man sitting with the help of a cane. He has bushy white hair and a similar white moustache which sways when he opens his mouth inhale air.

"Mr Pandey," I say louder, when there is no reaction.

"No need to shout, madam," he says with a scowl, finally turning towards me. "Nobody is deaf over here."

"Yes, sir. Of course, sir," I nod thrice. "How are you, sir?"

"Exactly how I was an hour ago. And you?"

"The same, sir, the same," I beam even more brightly. I see Pit Bull looking around for us and I catch her eye to motion her over.

"Miss Saroj, this is Mr Manoj, Aditya's father."

Beside me, Aditya chokes on his coffee but says nothing. Since I'd lowered my voice a little while introducing him, Manoj Pandey doesn't hear a thing.

Pit Bull smiles widely as soon as she hears that he is Aditya's father. Taking his hand, she shakes it so enthusiastically that I get a feeling it is about to come out of its socket.

"I am Saroj, sir," she says, still pumping his hand.

"Who?" Mr Pandey demands rudely. "Leave my hand, woman, before you pull it off."

She immediately drops his hand but her smile doesn't diminish even by an inch.

"Saroj, sir *ji,* Saroj."

"Manoj? How can you be Manoj? *I* am Manoj."

She laughs as if it is the funniest thing she has ever heard in her life. "I am not Manoj, Daddy *ji,* but Saroj."

Daddy?

Aditya chokes on his coffee again.

"Of course, I know you're not Manoj. Would you just stop screaming in my ears?"

"Ha ha," she laughs, a little nervous now. "I am Saroj," she says loudly.

"Saroj," he says grumpily. "Why couldn't you have said it in the beginning? Reciting Manoj, Manoj and driving me crazy like that…"

I lead her to sit next to him, "Maybe you would like talking to people of your age," I raise my voice to say to Mr Pandey.

Pit Bull, who is not a day over fifty, takes offence at my sentence.

"Don't you dare talk like that," Manoj Pandey says, waving a finger in my face. "You should not make fun of other people's age."

"Thank you, *ji*," Pit Bull says to him, pleased with his defence of her.

"You are very welcome," he says, blushing a little before turning back towards me with a scowl. "I am right, see, aren't I? Do I look that I am around this woman's age?"

"No, sir," I say loudly with my head bowed.

"Stop whispering," he says in disgust. "Speak up, young lady."

I straighten, "No, sir."

"Yes, yes. It is obvious how much older this pretty lady is than me," he says and Aditya choke on his coffee for the third time. I patt his back.

"But it is alright. I forgive you. Now, Miss Saroj, tell me how do you know Naina?"

Pit Bull still seems annoyed at the age remark but she finally answers, "She is your son's to-be-wife."

"My what?"

"Your son is going to marry her very soon," she replies, raising her voice even more.

"My son? You are very funny, Saroj."

"Thank you, *ji*, but why?"

Manoj Pandey guffaws loudly, "Ha, ha! My son has been dead for 10 years. Ha, ha!"

Aditya chokes on the poor coffee for the *fourth time*. Shaking his head, he puts the coffee aside.

"Your son has been dead for 10 years?" I ask Manoj with wide eyes. "Yes, I agree, that was really very funny."

"I am his grandson," Aditya quickly explains in a low voice to Pit Bull so that Manoj can't hear.

"Oh," Pit Bull's frown disappears and she turns back to Manoj. "Sorry, he is your grandson, isn't he?"

"My grandson?" Manoj pats his thigh and howls even louder. "My grandson is 11-years old!"

"Your grandson is 11-years old?" I ask in surprise and again pat Aditya's back because he looks really irritated. "Have you heard anything funnier than that?" I laugh too. "An 11-year old grandson? How absurd! Ha, ha, ha!"

"Naina," Aditya groans but I am having too much fun to stop. "It is alright, Uncle Manoj, you can tell Saroj."

"Tell me what?" Saroj asks.

I lean towards her and explain in a voice confessing a terrible secret, "His son was the one who'd organised a bomb blast in Delhi from Pakistan. So whenever anybody asks about Aditya's Daddy, he says that he has been dead for 10 years."

Saroj's eyes widen, "Really?"

"Yes, of course," I say innocently. "Would I lie to you? Of course not." I point to my face. "Do you think I am lying?"

She shakes her head from side to side.

"I can see you don't believe me," I say sadly. "Aditya darling, tell her about the time when you were three-years old and your Daddy still lived with you. Tell her what he got you for your birthday?"

"What?" Aditya asks warily.

"Oh, don't you remember? It was the day he'd been released from prison for allegedly murdering that waitress!"

Aditya closes his eyes and mutters, "I need a Scotch."

"No, darling," I say with a sweet smile, "Don't hesitate. Tell them."

He glowers at me, "I am afraid that I have forgotten. Darling," he adds with a sweet smile of his own.

I refuse to let him daunt me. "His Daddy got him a...a..." I think quickly. What would a terrorist get his son? "...an AK-47! *Now* do you remember, Aditya?"

"No," he says flatly, "I am afraid not."

"Don't worry," I say confidently to Saroj. "Adults very often cannot remember horrifying memories of their past. It is a natural defence their brain has."

"Oh," is all that Pit Bull can manage.

"Isn't it a miracle that Aditya hasn't been scarred for life?" I glance at my betrothed and bat my eyelashes innocently.

"Miracle," Saroj agrees in a whisper.

"Hey," Mr Manoj interrupts in a loud voice. "What are you three talking about?"

"Your dead son, sir. I am very sorry for your loss."

He snorts, "I am not. A piece of filth he was, nothing else. Even as a child, he was very interested in guns. Don't know what would have happened if he hadn't died in the encounter with the police officer."

There are goosebumps on her arms as Saroj pats his shoulder in comfort.

"You know, Saroj," he continues loudly, "if you didn't have the irritating habit of speaking so loudly, I would have really liked you."

She removes her hand, "Oh, really?"

"Yes, yes, even the dead could hear you, whereas *I* am a man with excellent hearing. You know, I can hear the wind rustle the leaves."

"You can?" I ask, not even pretending to be surprised.

"Yes, yes. Doctors are always amazed when they look at my ears. One in a million, they say to me. One in a million."

"Definitely one in a million," I whisper sarcastically.

Aditya pulls me up, "Let us go, Naina. Have fun with Mr Manoj, Ms Saroj."

As soon as we are out of earshot, the whole scenario strikes me as hilarious and I burst out laughing.

"Did you see her face when I told her about your Dad?" I laugh even harder. "Oh my God, that was priceless," I mimic her, "I am very sorry for your loss, Daddy *ji*."

His lips twitch but Aditya tries very hard not to laugh, "You shouldn't have said that."

"And the way you choked," I continue, ignoring him. "I am *so* evil."

"That you are."

We occupy our previous chairs at the bar and the steady flow of drinks restart.

"You have to drive home," Aditya warns me, sticking to his coffee.

"I'll ask Shaurya to pick me up, don't worry."

"Alright."

"By the way, did I tell you about this new guy I met at McDonalds' recently?"

"So now you're picking up guys at McDonalds'. Very classy."

I impatiently brush a strand of hair from my eyes, "Yeah, but did I tell you about him or not?"

"Nope."

I smile, dreamily, "His name is Vishal and he has the most incredible smile…"

"Really."

"Yep. We've met only twice and he hasn't asked me out yet."

"Strange."

"I know," I say and take one more sip, "Are you alright? You sound weird."

"Never been better."

I am genuinely confused, "Were you being sarcastic?"

"Sarcasm? Never heard the word."

I give him a cross-eyed look, "You know you're very strange, right?"

"People say so every day," he replies in a flat voice.

I shrug at his behaviour and finish off my nth drink of the evening. We sit in silence for a few moments and I look around the room. I'd forgotten my hostess duties totally, but of course, that had been just a ruse so that Fishman could stay close to me the whole time. Now that Fishman himself is in the Burns Unit of some clinic, the managers of the other departments are handling things, which was fine by me.

A few chairs away, I see a handsome man in his early thirties nursing a Martini and glancing my way.

The alcohol in my body makes me feel flattered by the attention and I smile. He smiles back and we check out each other for another couple of seconds.

"Don't do that," Aditya says.

"Don't do what?"

"Smile at that stranger. Do you know what happens to women who pick up strangers in a bar?"

"I am not going to *pick* him up, for heaven's sake."

"If you continue smiling at him like that, he'd come over, buy you a drink and half an hour later, would ask you to his house. You are going to refuse and he'd force you. In the end I would have to kick his ass for pestering you and I am not looking forward to that right now."

"Don't be absurd. A drink doesn't always lead to a nightcap."

"It does when a man sees a beautiful woman who is willing and drunk."

My pulse kicks in at the word beautiful and I laugh nervously to cover it.

"Jealous?" I ask, deliberately tilting my head in amusement.

He doesn't miss a beat, "Pea green."

I bite my lip in shock and tilt my head, "Well, you're not that bad yourself."

"Gee, you just made my day. Please don't stop."

"No, really. Remember I told you that Sanjana wanted to hook up with you? She thinks you're really hot."

He raises his brows but does not reply.

"In fact, my whole family thinks that I should stop the stupid man-hunt and marry you instead."

"Crazy," he continues in his bland voice. "Every last one of 'em."

Something twists inside my stomach at his sarcasm. "Exactly."

A few moments of silence descends. "We would probably be the worst-matched couple in the entire world," he finally says.

"I agree. Until two hours ago, I wasn't even sure about liking you."

A corner of his mouth turns up, "I liked you from the first day."

"You did not!" I say hotly.

"I did too."

"You called me lizard's tail and dog piss the first day we talked."

"Hey, don't put the blame on me. You first threatened to break my legs, destroyed my evening, and on top of it announced that I was an unformed foetus and a ball of snot.

How else was I supposed to react?"

I cover my mouth with my hand in disbelief. "Was I that crazy?"

"Crazier."

"It is a wonder you didn't dump Vandana that very second."

"It took me a little longer than that to come to my senses."

"But you still like me?"

"You asked a man the colour of his underwear and made him choke on his food. Do you know how much money people would pay to see that kind of entertainment? I got it for free. Of course I liked you."

"You're awful."

He flashes a grin, "I am, aren't I?"

"But that still doesn't change the fact that we would be awful together," I say and his smile disappears slowly.

"True. We would probably kill each other off by the first week."

"Right…"

"It is not that you are not handsome," I feel compelled to add. "God knows, you're gorgeous enough. And you are one of those very few people who like my warped sense of humour. Moreover, you do not back down in a fight, but instead are always willing to lock horns. My family loves you but…"

"But still we would not match," Aditya says matter-of-factly for the twentieth time.

"Vandana would kill me if I were ever stupid enough to go out with you," I say and immediately bite my tongue.

He seems surprised, "Of course she won't. We're good friends, nothing more."

I give him a patronising smile, "You won't understand. It is a girl thing."

"No, I insist. I want to understand."

"A best friend's ex is off-limits. Off-limits like *off-limits*," I wiggle my brows to emphasise the word. "A territory best not treaded upon."

"Don't be absurd."

"I am not. Didn't your sister explain these things to you? This is like the code of honour every girl is born knowing. You boys must have such rules too, like not making fun of the best friend's girlfriend/wife."

He ponders over it. "My sister and I were never close like you four are."

I am surprised, "You weren't?"

"Nope, not ever. Firstly, there was this huge age gap between us. However, I think it was more than that. My Dad was from a middle-class family, but he had always dreamt big. When anyone told him to stay back on the ground and stop fantasising, he replied that he was nothing without his dreams. He was a brilliant student. Class topper, school topper, university topper and district topper. He was so sure that by the time he would be forty, he would be in league with the Ambanis and the Tatas. It never happened. He got a degree and became a doctor but he was more interested in business. Real estate, architecture – tried everything except reopening his clinic. Don't get me wrong – we never starved but we didn't exactly live in luxury, either. Growing up, both my sister and I felt the pressure. Do better, always do better. Ninety-eight per cent wasn't enough. Nine-nine per cent wasn't enough. Both of us spent our childhoods with our nose buried in books. We never had time for friends or family."

I frown, "That is awful! I am sorry, I didn't mean it that way."

He smiles, "No, don't be sorry. You're right. It was awful, really. But we never had the time to realise that. We wanted to fulfil our father's dream and whenever we felt like giving up, he was there to inspire us. It wasn't that bad. So, even though I love my sister and I know that she loves me back, we aren't that close. What is done is done, I think, but I try not to let the past affect my relationship with her kids. Both the girls are awesome."

I smile, "My case was exactly the opposite. All four of us were born within months of each other. When I was due, Aunt Nandini announced that she was pregnant. Soon after Shaurya, Aunt Nandini became pregnant again with Manya and a couple of days before Manya's delivery, Mom became pregnant."

"Four toddlers at the same time? It is a wonder your house is still standing."

"I know. And even though all four of us are as different from each other as four people can be, we'd do anything for the other. While other girls in my class hung out with their boyfriends or girlfriends, we hung out with each other and Vandana. But even then, it wasn't always a big happy family. Some of our quarrels are legendary."

"But, of course, the good parts weighed out the bad ones."

"Definitely. Growing up was like a constant party. In school, we had our exams almost during the same time, so we studied together and the night before the exam was saved for relaxing. During that time, we just turned up the music very loud and hummed to it. Every other weekend, we would wash our driveway. Dressed in shorts and loose T-shirts, the whole morning was spent in playing with water and rain-dancing. Whenever some other cousin came for a visit, he or she would often ask whether we were always like that. It was nice," I feel compelled to add.

We fall silent for a couple of minutes and I wonder why I always start telling him everything about myself at every opportunity I get. Why is it so easy to share everything with him?

"It is getting very late," I remark.

He looks at his own watch. It is midnight, "Yeah."

"I should probably head home."

"You're drunk. I'll drop you."

"You're drunk, too. But even if you weren't, you still couldn't drop me. What would the neighbours think? An unmarried girl coming home at midnight with a man who is not even her boyfriend? I would never live down the scandal."

"India seems so crazy sometimes after New York. But never mind, the window panes of my car are black," he smiles. "I came prepared. If IIT has ever taught me anything, it is that."

"And what about my car?"

"Ask Raju to drop it off tomorrow."

"That poor chap has already done so much for me. Such a nice man," I say wistfully. "I wish I could marry him."

"Hey!" Aditya says in mock outrage. "I was the one who thought of the brilliant plan. I don't see you wishing to marry me."

"We just agreed that a relationship between us would be a disaster," I remind him.

"That is not the point. The point is to soothe my deflated ego."

"Yeah, I bet your ego gets deflated a lot."

"Definitely more often than you think."

Something is changing, I think. New bonds are being created, or maybe the old ones are changing. Or maybe it is just my wishful imagination?

"I really should go home," I say again.

He gets up, "I can drive and I am going to drop you. No arguments on this one."

I make a face but do not say anything. Aditya talks to Saroj for a minute and then both of us bid goodbye to the hosts and he arranges for a waiter to take my car and follow his to my house.

It seems that I am going to reach my home safely when, on the way back, we get stuck in an enormous traffic snag.

Aditya keeps on honking the horn and cursing, and it becomes official: we are stuck.

"What has happened?" Aditya asks the person in the car next to us.

"A truck has apparently crashed into a red light about a kilometre ahead," he replies and Aditya curses again.

My head begins to ache because of the combined effect of the alcohol, the blaring horns, the polluted air and the headlights of cars of all colours and sizes around us.

My phone rings and I take it out of my purse.

"Mom," I answer Aditya's questioning look.

"Hey, Ma. Yeah, I am on my way back...there is an enormous traffic jam on...yes, the radio is right."

"How long do you think it is going to take you to reach home?" Mom asks, worry evident in her voice.

I turn towards Aditya, "How long?"

"At least an hour," he answers, "maybe even two."

"Who is he?" my Mom asks, her voice now sharp with suspicion and I mentally roll my eyes.

"It is just Aditya," I reply in a tone one would use to say, "It is just my brother."

Aditya scowls at me but I don't pay him any attention.

"What is he doing there?"

"All the top honchos of Delhi were invited there, including Aditya's boss who couldn't attend and sent him instead. Since it was very late, he decided to drop me."

"Oh, good then," she replies in a pleased tone. "Your father is going to be very angry because it is late but I hope that you reach safely. Keep me posted."

Aditya takes the phone from my ear, "Don't worry, aunty,"

he says in that soothing voice of his which he never uses with me. "If it weren't for this snarling traffic...let me talk to uncle."

"No!" I say fiercely but he just puts a finger on his lips and gestures at me to keep quiet.

"Hello, uncle, how are you? Yes, thank you, I am fine. We are stuck in a traffic jam, uncle, just fifteen minutes from your home. It is actually all her boss's fault. He insisted that she had to stay until the end and play her duty as the hostess. He refused to listen that it was getting late...Don't you worry, I'll deliver her safely. Yes, sir, goodnight."

"You're the most wonderful man ever," I say gleefully as I end the call.

"Tell me something I don't know," he replies with a smirk and taps his fingers on the steering wheel.

We reach home at 2:15 a.m. He wants to drop me off at the main gate but Mom is standing there with a torch and she just wouldn't take no for an answer.

"Son, it is the marriage season. Most of the roads are blocked tonight."

"But, aunty, I can't..."

"Of course you can stay. It will take you another two hours to reach your home."

"It is Sunday tomorrow."

"No matter. Come on in. I won't take no for an answer. You have done such a huge favour to us...it is only befitting that we return it."

My car is already parked in the garage and as soon as I get into my room, I pull off my big, heavy and itchy dress and get into my shorts and a holey T-shirt.

After settling Aditya in the guest bedroom and handing him a pair of Shaurya's pyjamas, I return to my own room, brush my teeth, wash off the make-up and go to bed. Three seconds after my head hits the pillow, I am fast asleep.

"Naina, wake up, baby," my mother's voice comes as if from a great distance.

"Huh…go away," I mumble and bury my head under the sheet again.

"You have to get up…"

"It is Sunday," I reply without opening my eyes.

She says something again and her voice sounds worried but the only word I catch is… "Something, something, Aditya, something, something."

I curse him to hell for waking me up after such a nice sleep, and try to get up. My head hurts, my throat is dry and there is an acidic taste on my tongue. It takes me a couple of seconds to realise that I have a hangover.

"What is it?" I ask, sitting up with some difficulty and holding my head with both my hands.

"Should I wake up Aditya? It is just 8:30 a.m. but yesterday night he'd said something about early morning guests…"

He'd probably said that as an excuse, I think but since I am awake because of him, it is only fair that he should suffer the same fate.

After quickly brushing my hair and mouth, I knock on the guest bedroom. There is no reply. So I turn the knob. It is open and I carefully step in.

The bed is in a mess. He is sleeping diagonally, the air-conditioning is on and only his face is peeking from the sheets.

Feeling mischievous, I raise myself on my toes and without making any noise, go and stand next to his sleeping form. He looks beautiful while he sleeps, I think with disgust. Forget drooling, he doesn't even snore or breathe through his mouth.

I pull the covers down and say, "Rise and shine – Ow! Holy shit!"

Aditya wakes up immediately and screams automatically on hearing me scream. "Ahh...why-what-thief-why are you screaming, woman?"

My face is turned in the other direction and covered by my hands. All the time my mind is chanting, *He is naked below that sheet. He is naked below the sheet. He is NAKED below that sheet!!*

Technically, I cannot be sure of his nakedness because I only get a glimpse till his navel before I had turned away but...

I peep through my fingers, "I came to wake you up."

He adjusts the sheet around his armpits so that he is covered from his shoulders to the toes, "Knock much?"

"Stop being a grizzly bear. I knocked for three whole minutes," which is a lie but of course, he doesn't know that.

He adjusts the sheet a little more and I notice that his ears are a suspicious shade of red. "Aditya Khanna blushing?" I say with a smug smile. "How *cute.*"

"Shut up. You gave me the scare of my life," he says, raking his hair. "Screaming like a banshee."

"Hey," I reply indignantly, "it was not me who is sleeping naked in another person's house."

"I am not naked. See?" he pulls up the sheet over his leg and I get a glimpse of Shaurya's blue cotton pyjamas. "I always sleep like this."

"Uh-oh."

He massages his temples and runs a hand through his sleep-rumpled hair, "What time is it?"

I sit down next to him, "Quarter to nine. Mom woke me up to wake you up, because you'd said something about early guests last night."

"I lied because I thought she wouldn't want me to impose."

"You're hardly imposing. Your bare chest is going to make Ria and Manya's day and inspire Shaurya. In fact, it is going to be downright a saintly act."

He finally smiles, "What about you?"

"I am just going to have nightmares about hairy patches of land. Pal, you've scarred me for life."

He lies down again, "Do you mind if I catch a couple of hours more?"

"Yep. I had to get up because of you. You're not going to go to sleep now."

"Witch," he says but he has already closed his eyes. "Go away."

"Why? I like watching you sleep."

He doesn't open his eyes but smiles, "Oh yeah?"

"Your mouth is closed and I like it much better that way."

He turns his face in the other direction but I can still hear the smile in his voice, "With you standing over my head, I won't be able to go to sleep. Thoughts of rape and murder would plague me."

"Me? Raping you while you're *asleep?*" I snort and get up. "You're not that attractive."

He raises his head a little and opens his eyes, "Is that a subtle way of saying that you're going to rape me when I'm *not* asleep?"

"Ha! Your wish," I say and move towards the door.

"Very much," he replies and covers his face with the comforter. "Turn off the light before you go."

I do as he says and pull open the door. Three people fall inside.

"We heard screaming…" Manya begins.

"We thought you'd killed him…" Ria prevaricates.

"Then Aditya said something about rape and we…" Shaurya puts in.

Shriya Garg

I just shake my head. Eavesdropping, that is what was happening. All three very likely had their ears pressed to the door.

"He is just sleeping, not dead," I mutter. "But if you want a glimpse of an excellent male chest, don't hesitate to wake him up. He is naked under that thing."

"Naina," Aditya's voice calls out from the darkened room. "I am awake and I can hear you."

"Good," I tell Manya and Ria, deliberately not bothering to lower my voice. "Now you won't even have to wake him up."

"Good morning, aunty," Aditya says, stepping into the kitchen where Aunt Nandini and I are preparing breakfast. Actually *she* is preparing breakfast while I am putting bread in the toaster.

Even though he has a stubble from the previous day and is wearing the same shirt he'd worn that night, he looks fresh enough to do a soap advertisement.

"What's for breakfast?"

"Who said you're getting any breakfast?" I ask, waving my butter knife at him threateningly.

My aunt shoots me a glare but he just grins at her, "Where do you get such impertinent servants from? I don't like her one bit."

I raise my brows at that comment and say, "We only give free breakfast to beggars in the slum in the next block. Oh, I am so sorry," I add sweetly, "I forgot you were one of them."

"Naina," Aunt Nandini reprimands through clenched teeth. "Ria went to his room five minutes ago and asked him to come down for breakfast."

Her eyes shoot fire at me. *This is why you're never going to get married. This is why!*

Aditya gives me a mock solute, "Touché."

I accept it with an exaggerated bow and ignore my aunt.

"What do you want for breakfast, my dear?" she asks him, positively exuding bonhomie.

"Actually, I usually have just an apple and a cup of coffee every day."

"No, no, that won't be acceptable. You're a guest here. Naina, lead him to the dining table and then come back for the fresh juice that I have prepared."

I put down my knife as my toast refuses to pop. "Hey, he can get his own juice. He is standing right next to it."

"Naina," Aunt Nandini raises her voice and Aditya intervenes by picking up the glass. "Don't bother with the tiresome formalities," he says to both of us. "Really, it is alright. I prepare my breakfast every day."

"You better," I say and carefully begin buttering my toast which has finally surfaced.

"Learn something from him," Manya quips as she enters the kitchen for water.

Aunt Nandini's eyes harden at Manya's innocent remark and she says, "No need to lecture your older sister. It is an advice that you should follow yourself."

Manya freezes, like she always does in such situations.

"Yesterday I went across the street to Mrs Singh's. Do you know what she served me for dessert?" She doesn't wait for an answer but continues her diatribe as she wipes the marble counter with a rag. "*Rasgullas*! She told me that her daughter had made them herself. Isn't she your age? Have you ever made *rasgullas*? No! You can't even make tea properly. Last week Bharti had made *idlis*. I felt so ashamed."

Manya just stands there with her head bowed. I feel a surge of anger at her. Why doesn't she ever say anything? Being a cop, one would have thought she knew how to defend herself.

"Why can't *you* ever do something useful instead of parading around in that ugly uniform? When boys are going to come to see you for marriage, how am I going to tell them that my daughter keeps a gun on her bedside? Do you know that a nice NRI man has chosen Bharti? And look at you. I have been cooking since I was in class eight. I had six brothers and sisters younger than me."

"And how much good has it done you?" I snap, unable to help myself. Manya tries to shush me but I shake off her hands, shooting her an angry glare. If she can't stand up for herself, then somebody else has to.

Aunt Nandini's head comes up. She had forgotten about Aditya and me.

"You say that you have been cooking since class eight," I say, taking a step closer to her. "I beg your pardon but my mother hasn't. She learned cooking only after her marriage was finalised. Yet I don't find that her food lacks anything. Your food isn't any tastier, and except knowing how to make a couple of dishes – which any woman can find out through a cookbook – you don't even make anything that special. As long as you are comparing your children, why don't we compare our mothers? Don't stop me, Manya, I think it is high time. Aunt Nisha spends her whole day in the kitchen. Her food is legendary. And *she* started cooking after college. Why can't different children have different interests?"

My aunt's chin comes up, "Fine, have different interests, but have good interests. How is becoming a policewoman in this Godforsaken city going to help her find a good man?"

I am so repulsed for a moment that I can't speak. She is an educated woman living in the so-called 'modern' city for twenty-five years. And thus is what she believes in.

"Is cooking that better an interest?" I ask.

She does not back down, "Yes."

I try not to say anything. I really do. I know it is not my place to interfere. But as I move to turn, I see Manya's downcast expression and feel my pulse triple. I whirl on my feet to face my aunt again.

"Did cooking help Bharti when her father was shot to death right in front of her seven years ago?" I ask derisively. "Did cooking help pay her bills when her mother went in coma soon after? Did *cooking* help her when Manya scored 94 per cent in Class XII Boards and she failed? You say that her training doesn't *help* Manya? If you had ever paid attention to what she does, you would have known how much of a difference she makes. Do you know that your daughter saved three girls from being gang-raped last week? Do you know that she put her life on line for a man very much like your Bharti's father only *yesterday*?"

Aunt Nandini opens and closes her mouth, like a goldfish gasping for breath. The veins in her neck strike out and I try to make my tone gentler. "I am not being cruel. I am just being true. If you removed your attention for a second from your precious son, you'd realise that you have a daughter who has a heart of gold. Do you know that every time you give Shaurya an extra scoop of ice cream, a piece of Manya dies right in front of you? Some day, some day, you'd realise your mistake and along with that realisation would come another one," I say and look her in the eye. "Sometimes, it is just too late to apologise."

"Naina!" my father thunders, who must have arrived on hearing the commotion. I hadn't noticed. "Apologise to your aunt this very second."

I look at the faces in front of me. Aditya looks like a deer caught in the headlights. And I know that look in Manya's eye. She is going to cry any minute now. Thank God for Ria who is standing next to her and has taken her hand. Ria is with me, I know. Even Shaurya is going to support me because he knows what his mother did was wrong. Mom's face is carefully blank but Dad and Uncle Sandeep are furious with me.

"One apologises for things that one has done wrong," I remark in a shaky voice. "I haven't done anything wrong. I merely stated the truth. It is not my fault that people find it offensive."

I turn my back against all of them and walk right out of the house. It is cold outside and I am just in a thin T-shirt. I don't have any money or even my cell phone, but I am still too angry to care. It is because Manya doesn't say anything that my aunt continues to exploit her. I remember this incident when she was in Class X. She had her Maths exam the next day – a fact she was terrified of – and some cousins had unexpectedly arrived. She had still one chapter to revise, but her mother wouldn't hear it. She made Manya help her in the kitchen for two hours while Shaurya played video games. It had always been like that. Even my grandmother was like that. Whenever she came over, Shaurya and I were given preferential treatment because I was the oldest child and he the only boy in the family. What use were the other two girls? They meant nothing, except more dowries.

I cross my arms to protect myself against the wind when I hear footsteps behind me. Aditya drapes his jacket over my shoulder.

"And to think that only a few minutes ago I was wishing that I had a family like yours," he says slowly.

I smile grimly, "I told you yesterday that we aren't always a big happy family. Fighting is a part of it. But don't worry about me; when I go back, it would be as if nothing ever happened. All of them, except Aunt Nandini, would forgive me because they know I am right. She would take a day to sulk, and by next day, she would be again fawning over Shaurya. Tell me, was it like this with you as well?"

He doesn't answer for a minute.

"So it was," I say.

"No," he says finally. "Both my parents loved us equally. My sister was the older one and I was the male child – both of us had one point over the other."

We walk in silence for a couple of seconds more to the park a block away. He buys me a chocolate cone from a Mother Dairy roadside vendor and I say, "You needn't stay with me. They are not going to say anything to you. Go ahead, I will be back in a minute."

Shriya Garg

"It is alright, I don't mind. Yum, I love ice cream in winter."

"Yep. You haven't had ice cream until you've had it in winter."

We turn back towards the house and Aditya says, "Despite all this, your family is very nice."

"I believe that the words you used yesterday were, 'crazy, every last one of them'."

He winces, "I was drunk."

"But I agree. They *are* crazy."

"In a good way."

I glance at him from the corner of my eye, "You think?"

I see a figure very much like Ria approaching us. A couple of seconds later, I realise I am right.

"What happened?"

She is panting but hands over my phone, "Your phone."

I take it, thinking it must be someone very important for Ria to have run this far.

"Who is it?"

She winks at Aditya but speaks to me, "*Vishal*."

I put it to my ear and mouth *goodbye* to her. She suddenly leans over and hugs me very tightly. "I love you," she whispers seriously and runs off. I smile. It was for what I did for Manya, of course.

"Hi."

"Hi." Vishal says with a smile in his voice. "Who was that?"

Beside me Aditya continues eating his ice cream silently. I motion to him to walk with me, "My younger sister. Please don't mind her."

"Was she teasing you?"

"Yeah. She thinks it is very funny that men have finally started calling me."

"Don't kid me," he sounds genuinely surprised. "Men didn't call you before?"

"Thanks for flattering me," I tease and look at Aditya, who kicks a stone against a tin dustbin on the roadside. Talking to Vishal lifts my spirits a little. "But, no, they didn't. I scare them for some reason."

"You? Naw, shucks."

I laugh, "Thanks again for flattering me. So, um, what's up?"

He becomes serious, "I don't know how to thank you, Naina. Teaching those children…it has changed my whole life. I now see everything differently. I told a few of my colleagues about it, and they want to help these children as well. We're thinking of starting an NGO."

"That is – that is really nice," a lump rises in my throat, and for a second, I almost forget Aditya.

"Each of us is going to fund at least one child's education. We're thinking of a name. Can you suggest one?"

"I'll think about it, Vishal," I add impulsively. "That day at McDonalds', when I first asked you to teach those girls, I had been so sure that you'd think me crazy. But then you smiled and agreed so easily. And you're handling it all so well. Even if the whole effort doesn't give us much of a result, I'd be eternally grateful to you. You're a nice man," I finish shyly.

"Nice? Just nice?" he chuckles. "I had earlier planned to give you this news in person, so that you could jump up and down with joy and then throw your arms around me in gratitude. Nice is not good."

I smile but do not say anything.

"So, do you want to meet me for coffee?"

"Coffee?" I ask and Aditya kicks another stone harder than before.

"Yeah," he replies. "So that you can express your gratitude. Wait, I have a better idea. Why don't we meet for lunch?"

"My lunch hour is not that big."

"Hm…dinner is a bit of a problem because I usually work very late. What about lunch today?"

I look at my watch. It was already 11 o'clock and I had so much work piled up because I'd been busy with that stupid party for the last two days. Plus, the fight with my aunt had already spoiled my day.

"I am afraid I won't be able to make it today."

"This is not fair," he says in a disappointed voice. "Then we can't meet till the next weekend?"

"I am afraid so."

"The lengths a man can go for a woman," he says in a suffering tone. "Fine. I'll see you next Sunday. Why don't I call you in an hour with the destination?"

"Sure."

"Take care."

"You too. 'Bye."

I end the call and throw my ice-cream wrapper in a roadside dustbin. "That was Vishal."

"You told me about him yesterday."

"I did? Oh yeah, at the party."

"Yes."

The house arrives and both of us silently go in. The scene that greets me is just as I'd imagined.

In the dining room, my father, uncle and Shaurya are propped up in front of the TV, their breakfast lying untouched in front of them as they stare fascinated at the screen. It is the India-Pakistan cricket match. Ria and Manya are sitting crossed-legged on the floor in the other corner and playing Monopoly. Mom and Aunt Nandini are nowhere to be seen.

"Naina!" my brother screams, "move aside! You're blocking the view – fuck! Sachin!"

Dad and uncle are too busy echoing his sentiments to bother reprimanding him. Sachin Tendulkar has just been run out by a Pakistani bowler. In India, it would justify killing, forget cursing

"Aditya?" Dad asks without taking his eyes off the screen, "You want to join us?"

Aditya shrugs and everybody makes space for him on the couch. "How much have we scored – what? No! That's not an out! *Stupid* umpire…"

What is it with Indian men and cricket, I wonder but that answer is too difficult for any woman to come up with.

"I am going into my room. Please, nobody disturb me until 4 o'clock with my lunch."

"Yeah, whatever," Shaurya says.

"'Bye," Ria and Manya say together.

Aditya glances over, sees the files in my hand and gets up too. "I forgot about my work. Uncle, I better get going."

"'Bye," I say but I don't think he listens because he is busy explaining to Ria and Manya why he cannot stay.

I shrug and start dealing with the work. Barely two minutes pass before there is a knock on the door.

"Who is it?" I growl and open the door.

It is Aditya. "My coat," he says and grins. "It is rented."

"Oh, yeah, sorry." I hand it over to him.

"Can I talk to you for a second?" he asks.

"Sure. Come in."

He comes in and as I close the door, I see Manya and Ria glance at each other in the hallway and smile.

"Do you know that statistically, in a city this big, we might never meet again after today?"

"What do you mean?" I ask and make some space for him on the bed.

"I mean, we don't work in the same building; our houses are in opposite sections of the city and we don't have any common friends except Vandana."

I raise my brows and sit down next to him, "So?"

"You're not going to make this easy, are you?"

My heartbeat increases. *Is he thinking the same thing I am?*

"I don't understand what you're trying to say, Aditya."

He takes a deep breath and lets it out, "What I am trying to say is that even though you think that we are totally unsuitable…"

My blood is pounding and my head is ringing. I look into Aditya's eyes, which are levelled at me and I realise that…that it is actually the phone that is ringing.

"You…your phone," Aditya says and fumbles for my cell phone, which is still in the pocket of his coat because I'd put it there while we were walking.

He takes it out and glances at the screen. His face becomes carefully blank and I see him swallow. "It is Vishal," he says.

I mentally groan and take the phone. I end the call.

"I am sorry. You were saying something?"

He gets up, "You know, I don't think this is the right time." He holds out his hand as if a couple of minutes ago, he hadn't made my blood pound.

I shake it just as formally and say politely, "I am sure we'd meet again some day. Till then, take care."

"Yes," he says and puts on his coat. "Goodbye. Have a nice life."

"You too." *You idiot.*

He walks out of the door and then out of the house without even glancing back. The jerk.

I am sitting in my cabin, completing some reports on my computer when I see a swirl of pink and black pass across the door.

I immediately jerk out of my chair, "Sanjana, stop! At least listen to me, I am so very sorry."

She ignores me and continues walking to the washroom. I follow her inside. "Now you're being unreasonable."

"Unreasonable?" she turns and asks me angrily. "*I* am being unreasonable?"

"Okay," I admit, "I shouldn't have said 'yes' about you having Aditya and then spending the rest of the evening with him."

"You also said that he is single."

"Yes, I said that because he *is* single. Both of us aren't even very good friends."

She gives me a look of disdain, "Sure didn't look like it."

"What do you mean?"

She faces the mirror and fixes her lipstick, "I mean that the whole office is buzzing that there is finally a man who can kiss Princess Naina and not turn into a toad."

"*Excuse me?*"

"I know. But you two looked as though you were glued with Fevicol."

"He saved me from Fishman twice. That was all."

"I was not angry because you let a really edible guy slip through my fingers. I was mad because I thought you lied to me."

"I didn't, I swear."

Sanjana turns to me and smiles and I smile back, but before we can say anything, my phone rings.

It is an unknown number.

"Hello?" I ask.

"Naina Didi?" a young voice on the other end gasps.

"Yes?"

"Naina Didi, I-I am Ashish. Lax-Laxmi has had an accident," his voice breaks at the last word and I stop breathing. "Pl-please, come fast."

Same day
12:20 p.m.

Ashish and I arrive at A.I.I.M.S. at the same time as the ambulance does. The paramedics take out the stretcher, and there I see a pale, lifeless Laxmi. Her whole face is covered with blood, her dress is soiled and on her legs there is a lot more blood and torn muscles.

As she is rushed into the casualty ward, along with me, her harried mother and father are running too. I wipe away my tears and try to speak past the sob that her body has evoked in me, "What-what happened?"

"A school bus ran over her," Ashish answers me. I'd almost forgotten him. "Ashish – wait outside, please."

I can see that he wants to argue, but seeing my pitiful condition, he doesn't. I want to hug him and tell him that everything is going to be okay – he and Laxmi were close friends – but all I can manage is a small shoulder squeeze. "This is no place for a child," I whisper. "I promise I'd let you know what happens."

We are stopped by nurses outside the operation theatre. "Please," she says, "we will take care of her from here. Don't worry."

Don't worry? How can I not.

I sink into one of the hard metal chairs as Laxmi's mother sobs into her husband's shirt. She looks as if her heart is breaking. How hard it must be for a mother to see her child like that.

I wish somebody would hold me like that. I stifle a sob, open my cell phone and dial Manya's number. Somebody needed to take care of the legalities and hospital fees quickly. Who else was better than my kid sister?

The phone goes directly to voice mail and I end it before leaving a message.

The light above the operation theatre blinks on. We sit there quietly.

"What happened?" I ask.

Her father answers me, "She was crossing the road – the one before our houses begin – and didn't notice the bus. She was running and the driver saw her too late. He miscalculated and ran over her legs. The doctor says that, that she has very less chances of l-living."

Her mother clutches the edge of her saree and cries in loud, heart-breaking sobs. Again I think about my plan of adopting Laxmi. I'd assumed that because they didn't allow her to get educated and abused her, they didn't love her. But now on seeing the naked pain on their faces, I am forced to wonder. Maybe it is the circumstances, the poverty, which makes them do that to their own child.

The nurse comes over then with the forms and the payment is to be made immediately. They glance at each other. Somehow I manage to stumble over to them and snatch the papers.

"Please, don't worry about these," I say. "I…I will take care of them."

Her mother raises her tear-streaked cheeks. In her eyes, I see the same gratitude that I have seen in her daughter's eyes.

178   *Shriya Garg*

This is the only reason I don't notice her hands immediately. They have been joined together in *namaskar*, which according to our culture is a position to pray to God, or to greet or thank our elders.

And a woman, the age of my mother, is doing the same.

"No please...Don't."

She buries her nose in her joined palms and I stand there, hopeless.

"You, you are a miracle," she sobs and I take her hands in mine.

"Not me, but your daughter certainly is."

And as we sob quietly together, two strangers joined in grief, I realise that I am certainly nobody to judge them, having never been a victim of such poverty. Thank God.

My phone rings as Manya finally returns the call.

"Naina, what happened?"

"Manya," I clutch the phone tighter, "Laxmi, the kid from my school, she's...she has been in an accident."

She curses. "Oh no, what happened?"

"A bus ran over her," I gasp out.

"Hold yourself together, honey. I know how much she means to you. I can't come over right now. I'm undercover and we're just about to bust the bastard."

"What?" I whimper and put my hand to my throat, trying to choke it back. She is right, I tell myself and take a deep breath, I need to pull myself together, but it is so difficult to.

"Don't worry; I am going to send someone over. Just...just...shit, I am so sorry I can't be there."

"It is alright."

"No, it is not alright. I'll see what I can do. Take care, sweetie."

I close my eyes and nod. That was my kid sister – so weak sometimes and sometimes way too strong.

"I love you.' Bye," she says and ends the call.

I wrap my arms around myself and do the most tedious work of all: waiting.

Half an hour later, I am still sitting in the same position, with no more tears but just numb. A nurse had left the operation theatre 15 minutes earlier but was evasive to queries. "The doctor is doing all he can. I cannot say anything else."

Manya hasn't called again and there is no sign of anybody else. Shaurya is in Gurgaon for a case of his, Ria is in college and I can't call any of the parents because except for my father, nobody knows about Laxmi. He was already unwilling to let me adopt her, but now, when Laxmi might not even come out of the operation, whole – if alive – nobody is ever going to let me associate with her. It isn't as they are bad, or lack compassion; they just don't see the point. I can count on monetary help from my family, but what about the rest?

I think of calling Vandana, but hospitals make her nauseous. She hates them. What is the point of dragging her through all this for a girl she hasn't even seen?

I fold my legs on that same hard chair and wrap my arms around my knees. Laying my head on my arms, I wish for the first time that I had some more friends. Someone I could call at such a time.

Then as if my imagination has conjured him, Aditya comes down the hallway in long, assuring strides, with a *hawaldar* in tow. I raise my head and watch in amazement as he comes and bends right in front of me, looking like my very own Prince Charming sent by Walt Disney himself.

"What is with you and hospitals?" he asks with a grim smile. "Why do we always end up here?"

180   *Shriya Garg*

I stare at him for at least a minute. I feel like I'm falling. *Woosh!*

And at that moment, when I launch myself into his arms, sobbing, laughing, I don't care that he is Vandana's ex-boyfriend and he is off-limits, or even that I hadn't even liked him very much until yesterday. At that moment, when my shoulders are shaking so badly that I can't even breathe properly, when all emotions combine and spill over, all I feel is a deep contentment. Aditya is here with me. The guy who has rescued me so many times already. Aditya is here and the world would begin rotating on its axis once again.

"Hush, sweetheart," he says, stroking my hair and trying to get up but failing because I am half on top of him. "At least tell me what has happened. Manya just called me up and ordered me to get my ass over here."

"Aditya…Laxmi…a girl…oh God…she is dy-dying in there," I choke and make a futile effort to wipe the tears off my cheeks.

He finally manages to get up and settle down on the metal bench beside me, his arms still around me, "Water? Do you want some water?"

I shake my head and then nod.

"Let me get you…"

I cry out as he gets up. I clutch his shirt, "Don't leave me," ashamed at my pathetic tears, but still unable to stop them. "Please."

"Yes, of course, I won't go," he takes out his handkerchief, and fighting my hands, washes away the tears. "Just don't cry so."

"Aditya," I say earnestly, and turn away to the couple in the other corner, suddenly desperate to make him understand, "Laxmi is their child. I teach her once a week. It is a study group kind of thing, except…except that these children are not from as pr-privileged a background as ours."

He nods and I wipe my tears. "You won't believe how bright she is. She absolutely *loves* Maths! You should just see the way her eyes simply light up when she gets an answer right – it is like, like seeing the stars twinkle after a starless night. She doesn't even know how smart she is. Last month, her parents had finally agreed to allow her to attend school, but now…now she'll never be able to…" my voice breaks again and even though I am trying desperately to swallow my sobs, Aditya puts my head on his shoulder and pulls me closer, finally understanding what I am trying to say. There, in the crook of his neck, I stop fighting.

"Let it out, love," he murmurs. "It is alright, just let it out."

That is the moment. When he calls me his love and holds me so close that I can feel his strong, erratic pulse. That is the exact moment I realise that somehow, somewhere, along the narrow, twisted way, through our stupid arguments and fights, through the laughter and anger and tears, I've done the most stupid thing of all. I have fallen in love with Aditya Khanna.

Same day
5:30 p.m.

"Aditya? What are you doing here?" Vandana's voice coming from far away slowly penetrates my drugged mind. "Forget that. Tell me where is Naina? Oh, Naina! Naina, baby, you look like shit."

I try to sit up straighter, but my back is aching because I have spent the past six hours propped against the uncomfortable wall. Well, actually, part of the six hours. The rest of the time, I was propped up against Aditya.

"Feel like shit too. Anything else?"

She ignores my reply and quickly comes over to hug me.

Shriya Garg

"As soon as we get out of here, you are explaining Aditya's presence here," she whispers in my ear and that is so typical of the deceptively shy Vandana that I almost laugh out aloud.

"Oh, Naina, why didn't you call me?" she asks, sitting down next to me and taking my hand.

I feel ridiculous. It is Laxmi who is in the hospital, but it is my relatives who are crowding in the waiting area. There is Aditya, Manya, Ria, Shaurya and now Vandana. My father had wanted to come over too, but I'd stopped him.

"I am fine," I say. "There was really no need. Already everybody is here. I feel as though *I* have been hit by a truck."

Vandana clucks her tongue and gets me a glass of water. From the other side, Laxmi's parents watch us with tired, old eyes. Nobody has come over for them.

And suddenly, all my feelings of ridicule vanish. I feel blessed.

"Naina, why are you crying?"

"It is not you," I answer her. "I am just so glad you're here."

"I know. I am, too," she hugs me and I feel like I am in Class IX again when I had no friend, and had saved her from harassment and she'd hugged me in gratitude. At that time, I had felt stupid. Now I feel glad.

"Thanks, Vanz," I say softly.

She pulls away, "Sometimes, I swear, Naina, I wonder why I ever became your friend. You can be *so* dense."

I smile and sniff my nose. When I sense Aditya standing beside me with a cup of coffee, I wonder – irrationally – why I can't be one of those women who look beautiful while they cry. Oh, female vanity.

"How is Laxmi now?"

"I don't know. The operation is still going on. A doctor

came out to give us a huge list of the dozens of broken bones, ribs and punctured lungs. The good news is that she is still alive."

Ria takes my hand, "Have you eaten anything?"

"No," Aditya answers for me. "I have been trying to get that sandwich down her throat for the past two hours but she refuses to listen to me."

"Naina," Manya warns, "you need to eat. You need to keep your strength up."

"But I am really not hungry."

"I don't care," Shaurya says and takes the sandwich from Aditya. He rips apart the packing and takes a bite. "It is delicious. Eat it, come on."

"No," I say stubbornly.

His eyes twinkle, "Aw, come on. Tell me, Naina, how does a lion roar? Wahr!" He actually – and I can't stress that enough, I am not kidding – roars. I open my mouth to protest and he fills it up. I roll my eyes and chew while the others laugh. "Nice. But I am still not hungry. And you people don't need to stay. I'll be okay. Aditya, you have been here for six hours. I think it is time for you to go."

"Why don't you let *me* decide that?" he asks lightly but firmly and I know that he is not going to go. I shouldn't be, but I am glad.

The doctors come out then and the sandwich is forgotten. They are still wearing their green masks and their faces look grim.

"We are sorry to have kept you waiting. I am Dr Prakash," an old, tired man introduces himself to Laxmi's father. "I led the operation on Laxmi."

"Yes, doctor, what is the news?"

"The bus ran over both of her legs. She may never regain the use of them. There has also been a lot of internal bleeding, in.

184   *Shriya Garg*

The operation is complete but your daughter is still in a critical condition. We cannot promise anything, but she is a young, healthy child. Miracles can happen. All you need is faith."

"What does that mean?" her mother wails in agitation.

"We cannot say anything. She is in a coma right now, and she may or may not come out of it. Just hope for the best."

The doctors start moving away because they are also tired, and do not say anything to our inane questions like, "What are the odds?", "How can we help her?" or "Will she live?"

There is a silence of two minutes, as all of us fear the worst and take time to regroup ourselves. Suddenly Aditya pulls out his phone.

"What are you doing?"

"Calling my sister," he replies, his lips set in a thin line. "Remember, I told you that she works here? Well, if they are not going to tell us anything, they would have to tell *her*."

Ten minutes later, a beautiful lady in a sari crosses the hallway to us.

"What has happened, Aditya?" she asks, the crow's feet around her eyes crinkling in maternal concern.

"Hey," he greets her with a hug and turns towards me. "This is Naina, a friend of mine. Her student has been involved in an accident."

Aditya tells her the whole story and Dr Anjali Mathur regards me with serious eyes. "Where is the bus driver?" she asks.

"He has been detained by the police," I reply, eyeing her long black hair and fair skin with envy. She is Aditya's sister. Of course, she has to be beautiful.

"Why don't you all come to my cabin and sit comfortably? I'll see what I can do."

A nurse leads us to her room where we are to wait for her. She is back soon.

"Aditya, what they said was the truth. I could bombard you with heavy medical words, but the gist of it is that she has suffered a lot of wounds and is in a very serious condition. Her chances of making it are not good."

I bow my head.

"She is not going to be conscious any time soon, because she has been heavily drugged. There is also the coma. You all might want to go back home now."

"No," I say immediately. Her parents also shake their heads.

"Naina," she says gently, "it won't be of any use. One of you might want to stay, but the chances of her opening her eyes are minimal. Even if she regains consciousness, I doubt if she'd be able to talk. You can come back tomorrow."

"I will stay," Laxmi's mother volunteers.

"Very well. The rest of you, please go home."

Aditya glances at his sister moodily, "Anything else you have to say that might depress me further?"

Anjali smiles, "The girls miss you. You have to drop by very soon, if you don't want them to run from the house and reach yours every time they are angry."

Aditya smiles, "Will do." He kisses her forehead and says, "Take care. 'Bye."

"'Bye. 'Bye, Naina," she adds and touches my shoulder briefly. I get the feeling that she knows me a lot more than I know her.

Our whole entourage moves out. Shaurya promises to bring Laxmi's mother some food and after giving me a hug, takes off in his car. Manya decides to drop off Laxmi's father and takes off in her police cruiser. Vandana insists on seeing me home but I refuse and she finally caves in.

"But I'll come over tomorrow," she promises before leaving. "Just tell me the time you're going to come to the hospital, and we'll come together."

My own car is in the parking lot and Ria and I decide to leave together. Ria excuses herself to grab a burger from the hospital canteen and Aditya and I walk together to our respective cars.

I take a deep breath and meet his eyes for the first time in the past four hours. I have no idea what to say to him. I am still reeling from the realisation of my feelings to come up with anything witty.

In the five hours that we'd been together, he had left my side only once to see that Ashish reached his own home safely. He'd been there like a boulder, silent and strong.

"Aditya...I don't know how to thank you."

"You're going to embarrass both of us, aren't you?"

"No, really. What you did today was above the call and duty of friendship."

"Just shut up, for once."

"O...kay."

We stand together outside my car and for the first time, the silence between us is uncomfortable.

He exhales deeply, "I know now is not a good time, but, I think you should know this, Naina." I blink. He tucks a lock of hair that has escaped behind my ear and my heartbeat escalates. I feel as though all oxygen from around me has been sucked.

"Naina, I...I..."

"Yes? You what?" I ask eagerly, wondering whether he has realised it too.

"I am going to Washington for three weeks for a business trip."

What?!

Take One More Chance   187

My heartbeat returns to normal.

"What?" I ask sharply. Why is he not what I want him to be?

"I won't see you for another three weeks."

"When are you leaving?"

"Tomorrow morning. I catch a flight at 3 a.m."

"Have a safe flight," I say in that same curt tone.

"That is it? I am going away for three weeks and all you have to say is have a safe flight?"

I cross my arms and narrow my eyes, "Yes."

He chuckles, "Well, alright." He then leans in and plants a chaste kiss on my forehead in a manner very similar to what he'd done to his sister only ten minutes ago. This makes me even angrier.

I am not his sister, dammit!

I unlock the car's door.

"Goodbye," I say.

He frowns at my behaviour, but doesn't comment, "Take care."

"Go to hell," I mutter but he can't hear me because the door is closed.

"Hey, wait for me," Ria pounds from the passenger's side and I flip open her door's lock.

"What happened? You look pissed."

"Don't ask," I say through gritted teeth. "Just don't ask."

Two days later, there is still no news. I sit in front of my laptop, trying to get my mind off Laxmi's condition and Aditya's conspicuous absence in the best way I know – writing.

"You accountants are a different breed altogether," Vishal says from the doorway. "Stop punishing the poor keyboard for the sins it hasn't committed."

I surface from the mindless reverie every writer goes into after being given a pen and paper and close the window containing my novel. I get up to greet him, "Hi!"

"Hi to you too! I heard about Laxmi," his voice sobers up. "How are you?"

I manage a humourless laugh, "I am fine. Can't say the same about Laxmi."

"Sorry, didn't mean the way it came out. I have already been to see Laxmi."

I rub my tired eyes, "I am sorry, too. It is just that I am worried about her. What did the doctors say?"

"Still holding fort."

I do not reply to that depressing statement and glance at the computer screen. "What did you mean when you said that us accountants are a different breed altogether?"

He gestures towards me, "Look at you. Did you know that I have been knocking on your door for the past ten minutes? I'd thought that you had finally committed suicide. But what do I find? I find you decked out in ragged but comfortable attire and hammering away on your laptop. Your sister says that the sound of typing hasn't ceased even for five minutes in the last four hours. Don't you ever feel tired?"

I smile for the first time that day, "I am dead tired. But I know that if I stop working, I would think about Laxmi. So I am trying to keep my mind occupied."

"I am happy for you, then," he says.

I smile at him absent-mindedly and glance at my phone which is still lying, the screen unblinking. Aditya hasn't called even once.

Suddenly, right in front of my eyes, the screen starts blinking. I jump to get the phone and see that it is an unknown number.

"Hello?" I ask breathlessly.

"Laxmi has woken up, Naina madam."

My disappointment at hearing a female voice evaporates. "I'll be there in a minute."

"What happened?" Vishal asks me, sensing my excitement.

I quickly grab a coat to protect myself against the November chill and am already out of the room before he gets the import of my words and lets out a cry of joy.

"Mom, Dad, Ria," I scream without pausing in my quest towards my car's keys. "Laxmi is awake. I am going to the hospital."

"I am coming with you," Vishal says.

I pause for a second and then slam the driver's side, "Hop in."

Thirty minutes later, we skid across the hospital's parking.

"Can I go in and see her?" I ask the nurse stationed outside the Intensive Care Unit.

"Her mother is inside right now. She will be out in two minutes. You can go in then, but only for five minutes. And while you're inside, please don't discuss anything that is stressful. Be sensitive to her condition."

I nod and seconds later, her mother comes out. She is crying, but upon seeing me, she smiles, "Go on."

I take a deep breath and step inside. The smell of medicines and vaccines that is unique to hospitals threatens to overwhelm me, but Laxmi, lying on a white bed, looking smaller and more vulnerable than ever with needles poking out of her arms and blood bottles lying next to her, gives me strength.

Her mouth is covered with an oxygen mask, but her eyelids blink once in recognition. There is a bandage around her head, with red blood stains on it, and similar bandages cover her legs, or whatever that has remained of them.

"Laxmi, sweetie, hello," I say and carefully touch her right cheek, the only part not covered in bandage.

Her mouth tries to form a word and fogs up the transparent mask but I shake my head, "Ssh… no. Don't speak. Just focus on getting better. Blink once if you understand what I am saying."

She blinks once slowly.

"Good, and don't worry about anything. Your parents are so glad you're okay. I want you out of this hospital and in the school that both of us had decided that day in another month. I went ahead and brought your uniform yesterday."

The machine that measures her heartbeat beeps once. The nurse immediately comes in. "What happened? I told you not to…"

I wipe the tears from my cheeks, "It was nothing. She was just happy. I'd let you sleep now, Laxmi. And just remember that I…I love you."

A tear escapes from the corner of her eye and falls into her hair. I smile for the last time and leave the room.

"Is she going to live?" I ask the nurse as soon as we are out of earshot.

"We hope so. The doctors are going to do another hip bone surgery today, and if she survives that, she is certainly going to live."

I hate injections. I have always hated them. Even when we were being taught how they ward off lethal diseases like cervical cancer and AIDS, I hated them. I am 25-years old and have such eloquent feelings. Laxmi is barely 12 and she is being fed injections for breakfast, brunch, lunch, supper, dinner and dessert. I feel engulfed by my own tears and clutch my stomach tightly.

"Naina – don't worry, everything is going to be okay," Vishal murmurs softly next to me. Nobody knows that, I want to say, but I know he is just trying to make me feel better, so I nod.

And when he tries to put his arm around me, I get up. "Please, excuse me for a second," I say apologetically and flee to the bathroom. I don't want him feeling bad on my account. It is not that he is not a nice man. He is, but at that moment, I want a different set of arms. That is not his fault. Just mine.

Shriya Garg

A brief overview of the next three weeks (they do not deserve to be properly written down, those boring days)

9th November

Laxmi's operation is successful. She is going to live. Vishal takes me out for a pizza to celebrate and Aditya still hasn't called.

14th November

It is Children's Day. I take the remaining children to visit Laxmi in the hospital, and then we go and visit the Red Fort. Aditya calls on the landline number when I am out. Ria tells him all about Laxmi's recovery.

When I finally manage to make Ria confess every word she and Aditya had exchanged, there is no mention of me anywhere. I go to my room and sulk for the rest of the night.

15th November

Laxmi sits up.

17th November

Laxmi eats solid food and manages to hobble around a little with crutches. I burst into tears on seeing her like this and tell Vishal my plans of adopting her.

"You're really amazing," he whispers and I flush.

Eat your heart out, Aditya!

19th November

Vishal drops by when I am teaching the children. He has brought over chocolates for everybody. I ask him whether he wants to stay, and he nods. We abandon the lessons for the day and instead take turns in telling children stupid stories – *The Dog with One Leg who Got Stuck in the Aeroplane* and *Mobbit the*

Hobbit that are the best received.

21st November

No one has heard from Aditya. Mom invites Vishal for dinner and Dad becomes very happy when he survives it unscathed.

Aunt Nandini asks for his *janam patri,* horoscope, drafted by an astrologer when a child is born, taking into account the position of various stars and planets and their alignments. I cough loudly over my food, but Mom merely whispers, "What is the harm in looking?"

Yeah, I bet that is what David Headley thought when he was targeting Mumbai for one of the worst terror attacks in the history of India. *What is the harm in looking?* He must have thought, twirling his moustache. *After all, it is just a measly city.*

As soon as he is out of the door, Shaurya, Ria and Manya begin dancing around me in a circle while the television plays, "*Mehendi laga ke rakhna...*"

Mom covers my head with her red wedding dress and starts crying, "What will I do when you're gone?"

I ignore them. Calling them irritating is like saying that the CPI-M is just a group of rowdy, unruly boys.

22nd November

Vishal takes me dancing to a bar along with some of his friends. He becomes a little tipsy and dances with absolutely no rhythm, but doesn't misbehave. We scream and jump until our throats ache.

I have a nice time until we're outside my house, when he takes my hand and kisses the back of it. I flee in mortification.

23rd November

I dodge Vishal's calls and learn that Laxmi is ready to be discharged.

24th November

Laxmi returns home. I wish to contact her parents about the adoption but something holds me back. I decide to wait until she is fully recovered.

26th November

The first anniversary of 26/11 attacks. Vishal keeps calling. I finally pick up. He apologises for his behaviour and I forgive him. He invites me to meet his parents the next day. I refuse. He insists and asks whether I am still angry. I give in.

28th November

I spend the day with Laxmi at my place and bury the phone under the bed. I know Aditya's flight takes off tonight. I tell myself that he is not obligated to call me to tell me how he is doing or even to allow me to hear his voice. We are not even really good friends.

It doesn't help.

30th November

A quiet dinner with Vishal's family who lives in Noida. His mother kisses my forehead as soon as I enter and announces, "She is just as beautiful as you'd described, son."

I throw a confused look at Vishal but he merely winks.

His house is overly pretentious, and so are his parents, who love bragging about their son. "Vishal was accepted here… Vishal did this…His boss is always so happy…yadda yadda yadda."

I tune them out and only pretend to be interested while in my mind, I am going over the plot of my next novel.

2nd December

Aditya is officially dead to me. He has visited Laxmi, but not bothered to even send a hello to me.

No more am I going to write these annoying little paragraphs just because he is not in them.

Really, I should be ashamed of myself. Pining over a guy like some randy teenager. This has got to stop now.

Now.

Shriya Garg

I sit in a chair next to the window and glance at the road, sipping hot chocolate. My breath creates a mist on the glass–pane and I wipe it with my gloved hands. It is twilight, and people are rushing home from office to their families. It is our boss's birthday, so we'd been released early.

It is so chilly. The winter has arrived, bringing with it the smell of warm coffee brewing in the kitchen and sunlight that feels heaven on skin because it comes out so rarely. Now you see people in the park, all covered up in layers of sweaters and scarves.

Couples must lie late in bed, cuddling because who would want to leave the snug comfort of your loved one beside you?

Yeah, you guessed it right. He still hasn't called.

I am thinking that somebody who could be this dumb about not seeing the treasure sparkling right in front of his eyes doesn't deserve me. I certainly shouldn't cry because the only man I've fallen in love with doesn't return the feelings. Look at Vandana. If she would have been this heartbroken after every break-up, she would have been in an asylum by now.

A light drizzle begins outside and from Ria's room beside me, soft music emanates from the speakers. I shake aside my musings and go into her room.

She is bent over her study-table, completing her homework.

"Hey," I say, sitting down on the rug, cross-legged.

"Hey," she says without raising her head. "How is Laxmi?"

"Better now." I hear footsteps outside and Manya comes in as well.

"I am bushed," she mutters. She is still wearing her uniform and I know she has directly come from work. In her hand is a cup of coffee from which curls of steam are rising,

"How was work?" I ask, picking up a cushion and settling myself comfortably. Ria pushes aside her work and gets up to open the curtain so that the tap-tap of the rain is more audible now. There is a fresh breeze blowing in, making the room chillier. So I pick up a comforter from the bed and drag it down to the floor.

"Hey, hey," Shaurya comes rushing in, talking indignantly and already dressed in his pyjamas, "Partying without me? You brats."

The song changes to a romantic one and Manya opens some chocolates that are lying in Ria's drawer.

The parents are in their own rooms and I really couldn't care. We know we have absolute privacy. We are just about to settle in under the single comforter when there is a knock on the closed door.

"Come in," Ria says and Vishal steps in. "I am sorry for barging in like this, Naina, but I tried your cell and your Mom said to go straight up."

My cell is lying in the other room.

"Well, it is alright. Come on in. Did you want something?"

Vishal looks at us, lying on top of each other under one quilt and something that looks like wistfulness passes over his face.

"No, I just wanted to hang out."

"Sure," Manya says, "you can hang out now."

"But you'd have to put up with us," Ria teases.

"Aw, my luck has always been so very bad," Vishal teases back. "But are you sure you won't mind?"

"Not at all," I say and he smiles. He steps over all the things that are lying between the door and the rug and Ria shifts, trying to make space for him.

"Hey, sit here," Shaurya says and gets up from his place

right next to me. I lift my head from where it had been lying on his shoulder and give him a steely look. He winks and Vishal settles in gratefully next to me. I feel a little awkward. The rug is not that big and we all had been sitting pretty cozily. Now, the right side of my body touches his left and more romantic songs continue to play in the background.

Ria adjusts the window so that it is partially closed but the soft tapping of rain isn't muted either. The heat convector in the corner continues to spew heat and the temperature in the room slowly progresses from chilly to warm as we sit there, laughing and talking and eating.

"Delhi is beautiful in the rain, isn't it?" Vishal asks, his eyes savouring the drops hitting the gravel outside.

"Everything is beautiful in the rain," I contradict and everybody smiles. Slowly, my spirits begin to lift.

Shaurya claps softly, "Well said, ma'am. I wonder how you always come up with such perfect quips. I am supposed to be the lawyer in the family."

Manya musses his hair, "Don't you remember that Naina was always like that? The studious, scholarly one. Do you know, Vishal, that when we were young, we used to give our homework to her and she'd do it happily."

"Why would anyone want to do that?" Vishal asks, incredulous.

"Said it gave her practice." Shaurya rolls his eyes.

I flush and say defensively, "It improved my handwriting."

"'Nuff said," Shaurya adds with another meaningful look.

"Hey, I have seen *your* handwriting," Ria defends me. "It looks like black ants in pain crawling across the page."

"We are boys. Our handwriting is supposed to be bad," Vishal says.

"Excuses, excuses."

"Anyway, we all do stupid things when we are young," I say. At this, everybody reiterates the worst mistake they'd committed when they were young. Shaurya had caught a cat that used to hang out around our old house by its tail and hung it upside down for two whole minutes because it had peed on the homework. Manya had run away from home and hid at her friend's house for six hours before fear of her mother's wrath brought her back home. Ria had called up a girl whom she hated in the middle of the night and when her father went to pick her up, she had said, "I am Paramjeet and want to run away with your daughter. She wants to marry me, too, but is scared of you. Please, dear father-in-law, give her the permission so that we can get married tomorrow."

"Oh my God," I choke when we are done with laughing. "You were in what? Middle school?"

"Class three," Ria says smugly, stretching her legs and draining her coffee.

"But then how did you manage to alter your voice?"

"A handkerchief. Plus, I ate three cups of ice cream and slept right in front of the air conditioner the night before so that I would have a sore throat."

"My God," Vishal says, his eyes shining in admiration, "you are a master."

"Sue me," Ria grins back.

"And what is the worst thing that you have done, Naina?" he asks me.

"Me?" I say, placing an innocent hand on my heart. "I was an angel. Always prim and proper."

There is a moment's silence and then all three of my siblings guffaw.

"Puh-leeze," Shaurya says, "remember the time when you used to hide great-grandmother's cane every morning before she woke up and she finally fell in a well looking for it?"

"And," Manya adds with another laugh, "the time when you pushed your mother's best friend's son who was three years older than you from the bed because your Mom gave him an extra chocolate?"

"And," Ria chirps, "when you made Mom fire the housekeeper because she called you a *laundiya?*" (a word literally meaning 'girl').

"And the time when you made Manya steal a chocolate from the grocery shop for a dare?"

"And when you made us get up at 3:30 in the morning because it was your birthday and couldn't sleep?"

"We partied and went to sleep again before the sun arose," Shaurya confides to Vishal, who looks as though he's been a sucker punched in the stomach.

Vishal joins his palms and bows to me, "Grandmaster Kashyap, your wish is my command."

I look at the other three coldly, "Thank you. Don't you ever get tired of making fun of me?"

"You would think so," Manya says, tucking her tongue in her cheek, "but it is always as enjoyable as the first time."

Their laughter is so infectious that I join in. Suddenly, a new song starts playing from Shahid Kapoor's last flick, *Jab We Met* and Ria jumps up. "Aw, this is my absolutely favourite song. *Tum se hi din...*" She sings along and then tugs at Shaurya's sleeve. "Come on, let us dance," she says in her best yoo-hoo voice and shrugs off her coat. Shaurya doesn't resist and hops up as well. Both of them do an awful imitation of Shahid Kapoor and Kareena Kapoor together and the rest of us sit there, making fun of their moves.

"Yeah, Ria, like that. Twirl her a bit more Shaurya," I clap and then hoot. "Ooh, baby!"

Shaurya tries to dip her and in the process drops her. As a result, she lands flat on her backside. Ria doesn't let that bother her and is up and dancing again in a second. That is Ria for you – always smiling, bubbling and falling flat on her face. Or, as in this case, her backside.

A faster song comes up from the same movie and Ria and Shaurya dance in circles, their hands and bodies deliberately out of rhythm. They make terrible faces at each other and just jump up and down. We continue passing our comments and clapping and encouraging them. After a while the song changes again and another comes up, a slower one.

Aaoge jab tum saajna…angna phool khilenge… (When you will come, the flowers will bloom).

"Oh my gosh," Ria squeals. "Another of my favourites. Come on, Naina, come join us."

Though I am not shy by any stretch of imagination, the thought of dancing like that doesn't sit well with me. So I just shake my hand in negative and say, "You continue. I am tired."

Ria puts a hand on her hip, "Hey, Mr Aspiring brother-in-law, come drag your shy bride up. See, she is blushing because of you."

I freeze at the word *'brother-in-law'*, but Vishal merely laughs and gets up. "Come on," he says, stretching out a hand to me and not noticing my expression. "Let us dance. This is a really romantic song."

I shake my head a little and try to smile for the benefit of our audience, "No, really, I am alright."

Vishal smiles charmingly, flashing a small dent in his right cheek. Funny, I'd never noticed it before. How could I have not noticed it before?

"Naina, pretty please, I have never danced with a girl on a romantic song. Please, I would be honoured."

I finally grin, "Oh, alright."

He pulls me up and starts twirling me on the tile floor like I am a spinner top.

"Whoa," I say and grasp his shoulders for support.

He winks at me and then dips me so that my hair touches the floor. I laugh and he tugs me up with just a little flexing of his muscles. Around us, I notice that the rest of them have cleared the area for our little performance and they are hooting. Ria cups her hands around her mouth and screams like a cheerleader. "Omigosh, you look *so* cute together!"

At that my smile wavers a little, but he is dipping me again, completely out of rhythm and I am too busy concentrating on not falling to pay that statement much attention.

That is the only reason I miss Manya's subtle glance towards the door as she blows the two of us a kiss. "Ria is right. You two are just perfect."

Wait, something is wrong. Manya *never* blows a kiss.

I am shocked enough to stop dancing. But Vishal doesn't notice my hesitance and he continues moving his shoulders and hips and feet to the music. He tries to twirl me once more, but my feet are planted firmly on the ground. As a result of his pushing and my resisting, both of us lose our balance and fall on the sofa just behind me. He lands on top of me, and his weight nearly crushes me. "Oomph," I groan.

He laughs and then rolls over so that we fall on the floor. As the sofa is not very high, our fall gets cushioned by the rug. This time I am on top of him. Everybody around us is laughing and nobody is helping us up, but I do not find this a least bit funny. Or romantic.

He is holding one of my hands and the other is braced upon his shoulder. His is on my waist. All I want to do is shrug off and get up as quickly as possible, but this is an awkward situation for both of us, so I try to laugh it off.

There is a knock on the door, "I hope I am not interrupting anything," a voice says from the doorway.

Aditya is standing just inside the room, his face wiped clean of all expression. I get a peek at Ria's and Manya's smug expressions and I know – I just *know* – that Aditya has been standing there for a long time.

I'm going to kill them. Just wait until I am done with them. They are going to remember Hitler's *euthanasia* as mere drops of water when compared to my hailstorm.

"Hi, Aditya," Shaurya says with surprise. "When did you return?"

Two days, six hours, thirteen minutes ago, I think. He looks so good standing in a full T-shirt and jeans that my resolution of treating him like just another friend wavers a little.

"A couple of days ago," Aditya replies without taking his eyes off me. It is then I realise that I'd frozen. Or more importantly, I'd frozen on *top* of Vishal. We must look a sight.

I get up immediately and brush off an invisible speck of lint from my sweater.

Why do I have accidents only in front of him? Did I even kill a goddamn ant in his absence? No, but as soon as he arrives, it is like the King Kong in me that comes out.

Wait, King Kong was nice. Correction: the *Godzilla* in me comes out.

"It is not like you think," I blurt out.

One of his eyebrows rises in cool indifference, "What is not?"

I hadn't believed that he had the power to hurt me more, but with those unfeeling words, he broke my already bruised heart a little more.

"What is not?" Vishal laughs at the silence in the room and pushes himself off the floor. "I am afraid you haven't introduced me to your friend, Naina."

Shriya Garg

My friend. Oh, that is right. I'd forgotten. Just a friend. Silly me.

"Vishal, this is Aditya, a business associate. Aditya, this is Vishal, my friend."

"Oh, come on," Ria playfully nudges me. "Don't be coy. We all know who Vishal is."

I know what Ria is trying to do. Trying to get a rise out of Aditya. She has this crazy notion that because I am in love with him, he has to be in love with me too.

"Ria, don't," I whisper out of the corner of my mouth but she ignores me.

"Aditya," Manya says, following Ria's lead, "meet our to-be-brother-in-law, Vishal Rai. He is a civil engineer. Maybe you have heard of him…"

All colour leaves Aditya's face and my heart throbs in reaction.

Can't he see the desperate lie for what it is? I am surprised that Vishal doesn't say anything. He just smiles a little. What lies have Ria and Manya been feeding him?

"My congratulations to the happy couple," he says, his lips barely moving. I stand there, frozen, as he looks at me directly in the eye. Though his lips are curved into a smile, his eyes are cold. I have never seen his eyes cold. Aditya's eyes are always warm. Welcoming.

If I didn't know him so well, I wouldn't have noticed the pulse ticking in his neck. It told me what the cool mask of indifference hid.

He turns away and leaves. Ria pushes me to get me in action. "Oh, he is such an idiot," she says in disgust. "Go, grab him."

And I start running – down the stairs, across the hall, out of the door, to his car.

"It is not what you think," I say but that little defensiveness has crept into my voice, making me sound guilty even when I am not.

"Go away, Naina," he says levelly, opening the car's door.

"Oh, don't you dare play the injured party now!" I snap, anger giving me the strength to block his body.

He raises his eyes to mine and they are not blank any more. Instead, they are filled with a raging storm. I realise that angering Aditya Khanna is not a very good idea.

Well, it is too late for that.

"Oh really?" he says with biting sarcasm. "And what do you want me to do when I see you dancing in the arms of another man who has no misconception about holding you in whatever way he wants when *I* haven't talked to you for almost one whole month?"

"And *that* is my fault," I ask, "that we haven't talked for one whole month? I wasn't the one who didn't reply to e-mails and forgot that there has been a new discovery – cell phones."

His brows draw together over his eyes, "So you went off and agreed to marry another? Very persistent, Miss Kashyap."

I put down my foot, "Oh, for God's sake, Vishal and I are not going to get married."

"I can certainly see that."

I cannot believe it! We haven't talked since ages and now that we finally are, it is because we are fighting.

"Vishal and I are just friends. I am sorry that because you didn't call, I wasn't with my pillow, sobbing."

He stops trying to go past me and clutches my forearm in a very painful grip, "I hate liars."

I look up at him, surprised and a little scared. What has happened to him? And then I see it – the hurt which he is so successfully hiding beneath the anger and disgust.

Shriya Garg

"Aditya," I inhale slowly, trying to calm my erratic heartbeat. "Aditya," I exhale, "I love you."

His expression doesn't change. He removes his hands from my forearms and uses them to cup my face. I've never said these words to a man and all he gives by the way of a reaction is silence.

Looking at me directly in the eye, he whispers savagely, "You are despicable," before putting his mouth over mine. I freeze.

A second later, he pulls away. His eyes are still narrowed, but I am too happy to pay attention. He is jealous. Of course, he is jealous. That is why he is reacting so coldly. It explains everything.

"Well, it is alright then," he says, his voice filled with the same disgust and my happy bubble deflates a little. "I don't mind so much now that you marry Vishal. Not when I am the one who would get the goods. First affair after marriage with me and everything," he sneers and I take a step back. The blood stops flowing in my veins.

"What...what are you implying?"

He smiles – a smile unlike the ones I've ever seen – and says, "I am not *implying* anything. I am saying flat out. It is of mutual benefit to all three of us."

I know my lower lip is trembling. I take another step back, "Aditya, if you're angry, just tell me. Don't say such... such...crude things which you are going to regret later."

He gives a one-shouldered shrug, "The only thing I am going to regret is thinking that I would have to marry you to get that delectable body. I was wrong. I am *happy* I was wrong."

I close my eyes for a second, praying for courage. When I open them, Aditya is still standing there, looking with the same contempt in his eyes.

"Do...don't ever," I say in a shaky voice, "come near me again. I hate you. Just get *out* of my life."

"Happily," he says and slides into his car. Whistling a happy tune, he lowers the window and says, "Have a happy life, Naina. May God protect Vishal."

Then without another backward glance, he races out of the parking, leaving me and my broken heart behind.

I sink to the ground and start crying, because that was exactly where I was, when he hadn't called – with my pillow, sobbing.

So this is my story.

Isn't it amazing how much it resembles those dumb Bollywood movies?

Vandana disagrees. She thinks it is not amazing at all. That my life resembles those dumb Bollywood movies, I mean.

The poor girl. She is worried about me. She thinks I am suicidal, just because I googled 'How to kill myself'. People use Google for such stupid things all the time. She doesn't realise that.

I have told her a hundred times that I am perfectly fine, but she just clicks her tongue and says with eyes full of pity, "Poor baby."

"You didn't want me and Aditya together anyway," I say angrily. At this, she tells me to sit down.

"What?" I ask.

"Just sit down, Naina. I have to tell you something."

I sit down.

"Aditya was never my boyfriend," she begins.

"Huh?"

"I was just match-making."

It takes me a moment to get the import of her words, "Huh?"

"After our first date, I thought Aditya was perfect for you. No, I *knew* Aditya was perfect for you. But I also knew that if I threw him across your way, you would dispose him off like you'd done with the others. So, I waited and I planned."

I blink.

"I pretended to be still interested in him so as to see your reaction. You never disappointed me. You have always been so obvious about everything. The whole world knew that Aditya was The One for you."

"The whole world?" I echo.

"Of course," she says, smiling. "I involved the three of them into it as well. They helped me nudge you in the right direction. The date with Nitin, the Diwali party, his break-up with me...Everything was choreographed to the last detail before being implemented. The way Ria told Vishal to ask you to dance, the way Manya and Shaurya encouraged, the way your Mom was conveniently reading Vishal's *janam patri* when Aditya came along."

"Wait – back peddle a little – what about Vishal's *janam patri*?"

"I know, I am sorry," she admits, "I shouldn't have done that. I had no idea Aditya would take it so badly."

"So badly?" I snort, the first signs of any emotion in the past three days. "God, when I think of the murderous expression on his face...I could kill you."

"I know that, honey, but I was just trying to help you out. forcing Aditya into confessing his feelings for you."

"You pesky little match-maker!"

"But don't you see," Vandana grins suddenly, "that means his feelings for you are stronger than any of us thought?"

The brief rush of adrenalin fades as quickly as it has come. "Vandana, he almost plainly called me a whore. That is what he thinks of me."

"I know and I could kill the jerk for that, but..."

"No buts."

She opens her mouth to say something but I shake my head, "No, I don't want to hear anything. Just leave me alone." I curl into a tight ball on the bed, "Just leave me alone."

For a second she doesn't say anything, but then she does as I say. Switching off the light, she closes the door and leaves the house.

I stay in that position, staring at the wall, thinking – thinking where I went wrong; what I could have done better.

Maybe I shouldn't have agreed to dance with Vishal. Maybe I shouldn't have fallen on top of Vishal. Maybe I should have tried to contact Aditya before this instead of just sitting angrily. Maybe…

Ria comes in without knocking.

"Knock much?" I ask, without raising my head. Even those two words remind me of him. When he'd been bunking here. The morning I'd seen him shirtless. I clutch the sheets tighter.

"I knew you wouldn't answer," she shrugs. "Come on, get up now. Don't just lie there so pathetically."

"I am pathetic."

"No, you're not. You're just dumb."

"Right. Everything is always my fault."

"No," she says sharply, "not always. Just this once."

"Of course," I say with only a hint of sarcasm, still staring at the wall.

"Aditya was *so* obvious. You'd go out of the room, his eyes would follow you. You come into the room, his eyes would follow you. Whenever you were around, he was always smiling. God, the guy took three men to the hospital for you! If you were even slightly hurt, he'd be out with a first-aid kit. When you talked to – or about – one of your stupid dates, his eyes would scrunch up and his smile would vanish. He…"

"Shut up," I say very quietly.

She gets up and glares at me angrily, "Why? Why should I shut up?"

"Because it is none of your business. You had no right to interfere in my life. You should have respected my privacy and wishes."

"You are my Goddarn sister!"

"And still you're taking his side?"

"Don't be nasty, now, Naina. This is not about taking sides. This is about your life. Do you know that Uncle Prakash has already made an appointment with some friend of his because his son is of your age and is looking for marriage? I agree what Aditya did was wrong, but he was hurt! And jealous!"

I close my eyes and pull a pillow over my head. The wounds are still too raw. "Go away."

"No."

"Ria, just leave me alone."

I hear her getting up. "Fine," she says loudly. "Do what you want. But remember, it is your life and since you don't want us *interfering*, we are not going to help you bring it out from the mess it has become! Don't come to us now, begging for help."

"'Bye."

"God! 'Bye! Go to hell!"

I don't bother to reply but try to go to sleep. I haven't gone to office for three days. Shaurya had called up my boss and told him that my great-grandmother had died. She had died eight years ago, but hey, he doesn't know that.

Still in bed. Haven't eaten anything since yesterday when Ria shouted at me. Nobody at home is talking to me any more.

Still in bed. Still haven't eaten anything. Still nobody is talking to me. I am probably going to die of the pain.

They must think I deserve it, after all.

Thinking of dying, I have an idea.

List #4: Best Ten Ways to End Your Life
By Naina Kashyap (With inputs from www.google.com)

10) **Jump off Mr Aditya Khanna's roof.**

Nah, I get dizzy just by looking down. I'd probably puke all the way down while going to meet my demise. I need a dignified end, not this.

Verdict: Rejected.

9) **Eat Mortein mosquito killer or rat poison.**

When they do it in the movies, white froth materialises around their mouth, which is just *gross*. It is like with young toddlers, when they eat soap. Nope.

Verdict: Rejected.

8) **Hang myself from the fan in Aditya's dining room.**

Well, he certainly won't be able to entertain any lady friend there after that. Hmm, maybe I'll try this after all.

Verdict: Keep for later consideration.

7) **Put the open end of the gun in your mouth and press the trigger.**

Oh, no, *way* too much of a mess. I saw this once on CD. My maid is going to curse me till eternity for making her clean up all the blood. She has this way of muttering all the time through the corner of her mouth as she sweeps the floor.

And isn't this what every girl wants? To be hated by your family, and even despised by your maid.

Verdict: Rejected.

6) **Stab yourself with a knife.**

Too painful. Somebody would definitely hear me screaming and take me to the hospital. And where would I be then? Stuck in the ICU with blood bottles and that nauseous smell around me.

But then, since everybody around me practically hates my guts, so they would just laugh as I would bleed to death.

I should consider this one. But do you become numb as the blood gushes out or does it still hurt?

Verdict: Research more on the subject.

5) **Drown myself in a pool.**

No, it is one of my worst fears. Drowning. I hated it when I thought Rishab was drowning and I hate the thought of drowning myself willingly.

Verdict: Rejected.

4) **Hold my breath till I die.**

I researched this and it has been scientifically proved that holding your own breath to kill yourself is impossible. Thank God.

Verdict: Rejected.

3) **Make a crude bomb (it tells you on the internet how to) and explode it right beside me.**

Well, such a dramatic exit would definitely make my family remember me. I can almost imagine that ten years down the lane, when the whole family would sit down for dinner and Ria and Manya's little kids would ask about me, "Mommy, who was Naina? I heard the name in the news."

(Yes, they wouldn't have told their kids about me. They would have to hear it from the *television*, to boot.)

"Oh, Naina?" Ria would ask, trying very hard to remember. "Oh, she was just a crazy aunt who made a bomb and blew herself up. We had to move out of the house after that. Looked so ugly."

"With the pieces of her dead body lying around?" my cute little nieces and nephews would ask.

Manya would laugh, "Oh, don't be silly, I was talking about the fact that there was smoke coming out of one part of the house, very much like the Taj Hotel looked on the night of 26/11."

Verdict: Research more on the subject.

2) Electric shock.

I remember getting one when I was very young and had shoved my pinky finger into an electric outlet. It was this *buzzy* feeling that shakes you from the top to the bottom of your soles.

But an electric shock powerful enough to kill you...doesn't sound so good. Plus, my hair will stand up and wouldn't I look ugly then, lying with that haircut in my coffin? Shudder.

Verdict: No, please. Rejected.

1) Take sleeping pills.

Nice. Clean. Smooth. Just a bottle of pills and go to sleep. There is one on the internet that promises that it would never wake you up. *A sleep to the afterworld*, it says proudly. You can order them online and they offer to deliver it right at your doorstep in two days.

My, but who would have thought that the internet was so resourceful?

Verdict: Approved.

The pills have arrived. Mom has left the brown packet outside my door. Thank God she didn't see what was inside.

I stretch my head from side to side and open it.

Whoa. Pretty pills. They look so harmless.

I stretch my fingers and pick up a pen to conclude this splendid piece of work.

My dear friends and family,

I dreamed I was missing. I was so scared, I called out but nobody cared.

And after my dreaming, I woke up with this fear, what am I doing here?

So if you're asking me, I want you to know that my time has come.

Forget the wrong that I have done. I hope I have left behind some reasons to be missed. Don't resent me and when you're feeling empty, keep me in your memories. Leave out all the rest.

Don't be afraid. I have taken my beating. I have shared what I've made. I am strong on the surface, but not all the way through. I have never been perfect, but neither have you.

I probably could have done with better friends and family, but beggars cannot be choosers, right?

I don't think I would miss you, but still...

I'd miss you.

Goodbye.

Well, alright, I accept, it is actually a modified version of Linkin Park's '*Leave out all the rest...* (splendid song by the way), but nobody in my house listens to Linkin Park, anyway. Let them think that it is just a product of my wonderful creativity.

10:00 p.m.
There, I am done.

I have thrown all my clothes and accessories in a carton and tagged them for my various students and charities. My books have been left for Aditya. A nasty reminder, I am sure, it is going to be. Tee hee hee!

So, I guess, cruel world, this is it. The ending. I have taken out the pills and am ready to go to bed.

10:30 p.m.
Deep sigh.

11:00 p.m.
Opening the cork. Slowly, slowly.

11:15 p.m.
Taking at least twenty of them in my hand.

Again a deep sigh. And… swallow. Mm…these are *tasty*…

11:30 p.m.
Dying…
Dying…
Thud!
Dead.

R.I.P. Naina Kashyap.
Beloved daughter, sister and friend.

6:30 a.m.

Well, no, I am not dead. Obviously.

I don't know what is happening. Those pink capsules taste just like my favourite candy. And except for the slight sugar rush, there is no other effect either. So, I sit cross-legged on my bed, thinking, *am I dying? Am I dying? WHY AREN'T I DYING?*

Suddenly, the door opens and Manya barges in with a militant expression on her face.

"I am," she speaks through clenched teeth and I cringe, "ashamed of you."

"What have I done *now*?" I wail.

She waves some white pills in front of my face, "What have you done now? *What have you done now?* You were going to kill yourself! You little coward! Do you know when I was young who I wanted to be like?" She doesn't wait for an answer but continues, "You! You, with your strength and that knife of a tongue which could put any person in his place, from a thug to a toddler. Do you have any idea what would happen if I just as much as *hinted* of your little stunt to Uncle Jai? Or Aditya?"

I lower my face.

My mind has stopped working. *Aditya, Aditya, Aditya,* it is chanting, *would probably jump with joy.*

And with that statement, the full import of what I'd been going to do sinks. And I start crying.

"Why, Naina, why?" she asks, shaking me. "Why this? Thank God I'd seen the delivery and replaced the pills with the candy. But why?"

The dam inside me breaks. How do I explain to her how it feels? Feeling unwanted?

"You have barely eaten in the past week. You have lost so much weight. Your hair is a mess and your face looks as though it has never seen water. There are dark circles under your eyes and you look pale to the brink of death. And I hate to say it but, Naina, you stink."

At this, I sob even louder. Vain, even in death.

I've wanted just one thing in life. One. And how do you feel when even that wish doesn't get answered? When you lie awake in your bed but you're not awake at all and all your thoughts lead back to one certain person. Whether he is thinking of you now...whether he thinks of you *at all?*

"I think this has gone on long enough," Manya says with steel in her voice. She gets up and opens the door. I pause long enough from my crying jag to see the person standing outside the door, looking even worse than I am feeling.

"You can go in now, Aditya. And if you break my sister's heart once more, I'd make sure you spend the rest of your life hauling shit in jail."

"Aye, aye, ma'am," he says with a ghost of a smile and steps in, locking the door behind him. Everything inside me stills as I watch him make his way towards me.

"Can I just," he begins in a hoarse voice, "hold you for a second? I promise we'll talk later."

My heart knows that I want to go. I want to go *so badly.* But my head is showing me images as though in a movie... *"I don't mind so much now that you marry Vishal. Not when I am the one who would get the goods. First affair after marriage with me and everything..."*

"I am not implying anything. I am saying flat out. It is of mutual benefit to all three of us..."

"The only thing I am going to regret is thinking that I would have to marry you to get that delectable body. I was wrong. I am happy I was wrong..."

"Have a happy life, Naina. May God protect Vishal..."

I shake my head mutely.

He sighs and a corner of his lips curves upwards in a morose smile. "I hadn't expected a 'yes' anyway," he says.

It is the first time that I have seen him look so unkempt. His hair is mussed as though he'd raked his fingers through them one too many times. There are stains on his T-shirt and his jeans looks shabby too.

There are hollows beneath his eyes and as he raises his hand to rake his hair again, I notice that his fingers are trembling.

He slowly sits down next to me on the bed, close enough to touch but still far away.

"Naina, I know I hurt you that day."

I turn my face in the other direction because I don't want him to see my face which crumples up every time that day is mentioned.

"Please look at me," he says quietly and motions to take my hand in his. I anticipate the action and remove my hand before he can touch it.

"Do I repulse you that much?" he asks. There is no judgement in his voice, just an inquiry.

I do not reply and continue meditating on the opposite wall.

A couple of minutes of silence later, he tries again, "Manya told me what you were going to do."

My fingers clench and unclench the bedsheet, but I continue maintaining my silence.

"With those pills. Naina...I..." his voice trembles slightly and then quickly recovers, "I should be furious with you. But I would be a hypocrite if I said that I am furious with you, because you see, even though I do not think of myself as a quitter, that thought did cross my mind too."

I finally turn towards him.

"Funny, isn't it, how you get to know that you aren't strong at all when you need the strength the most?" he says with a self-deprecating smile.

He leans forward as though pulled by some external force and tucks a strand of my hair which had escaped behind my ear. "When I was in Washington, I would have traded my soul for the sound of your voice. But I was swamped with work. It was actually a four-week trip, but I convinced my boss to cut back on seven days if I managed to finish the work in three weeks. Added to the time difference, there was no decent hour when I could call you. I got only one opportunity and when I tried your cell, it was switched off. When I tried the landline, Manya told me you were out with someone."

With 13 little children. Damn you, Matchmaker Manya.

"And when I got back...An idea struck me and I began preparations immediately."

He looks at me expectantly. I merely raise my eyes and read the disappointment there.

"What...idea?" my voice is rusty from lack of use but he doesn't seem to notice it. Because as soon as I ask that question, he puts his hand in the pocket of the jeans and takes out a satin box which is not even as big as my palm.

"That day when I came over and saw your mother matching yours and Vishal's *janam patris* and then you lying in his arms, laughing while everybody cheered...I....Naina, I, simply went mad. There are no other words. It wasn't jealousy, because I've already felt that emotion every time you used to talk about Vishal. No, it was something much more... something hotter, more consuming. All rational thinking vanished at that time. And I hurt you. I hurt you because I wanted you to feel what I was feeling. I am sorry, Naina. I love you. It is perhaps the worst excuse I could have thought of for what I did, but it is still true."

A tear drops from my eye and I impatiently brush it away, "Why did you come here today?"

If he notices that I haven't said anything in response to his earlier comments, he doesn't say it. "I actually came yesterday. I was going crazy without you. Vandana took pity on me and told me about Vishal and how you met him because of the children you teach. I grabbed the life-line for what it was and immediately came over. It was 10 o'clock, yesterday night. Manya told me about the pills and how she'd replaced them. She made me wait outside because she wanted you to get ample time to go over the consequences of what you'd done as you waited for the death that would never come. I waited eight hours. And you know what I learned in those eight hours?"

"What?"

He shakes his head slowly, "That you've got to love me too. Why would you even think of ending your life otherwise?" He gets up and comes to stand in front of me. "So, Naina Kashyap," he begins and kneels on the floor so that we are almost at the same level with him on the ground and me sitting on the bed, "I once told you that I'd never kneel before a woman," he says solemnly, without a hint of a smile. "I take back my words."

I stop breathing.

"I promise to love and cherish you forever," he says in his most earnest voice. "Till death do us part." He opens the ring box to reveal the most beautiful thing I've ever seen, next to him, of course.

"Will you please, please, marry me and make me the happiest man in the world?"

I have never seen him so serious. His eyes plead to mine. I do not say anything. They beg. And I can't hold myself back any longer.

"Yes," I whisper.

He gets up in slow motion, reeling from the shock. Then he starts laughing. Falling on the bed, he hugs me so tightly that for a moment I'm afraid my bones would break.

"Wait – there is one more thing," I say before I am too far gone for any coherent thought.

He pulls back, his eyes wary, "What?"

I lower my eyes, "Aditya, I want to officially adopt Laxmi."

He doesn't say anything and I hasten to add, "I know that she is not what you might have expected our first child to be. She is very old and a part of her background, her misery, would always stay with her. But, Aditya," I finally meet his eyes and plead to them, "she is the most exquisite child I've ever had the pleasure to meet. She is....beautiful. And I promise that I accept full responsibility for her. I know everybody thinks that I am not mature enough to handle a girl as old as her, but I'll manage. And there is also the matter of our parents and other relatives, but...I love her, Aditya."

He still doesn't say anything and continues looking down at me, his face expressionless. I place my palms on either side of his head. "Do you think that you might be able to love her a little, too?" I whisper.

He finally smiles, "Naina, I would love any child you give me."

I clutch his head tighter, afraid to believe that all of it is true, "Really?"

He takes my palm in his and places a kiss in the middle of it. Then he gazes directly into my eyes and his eyes look so deep that I could drown in them. His throat seems a little clogged and he has to clear it twice before I can understand what he is saying.

"I will be *honoured* to raise her up with you."

I burst into tears. He wipes my tears. "Naina," he says, clearing his throat, "do you promise to love me forever?"

I nod, "Yes."

"Through high hell or water?"

I nod slowly, wondering what he was getting at, "Ye-es?"

"No matter what I say or do?"

"Yes?"

"Naina, I love you, but…"

"Ye…e…es?"

"You stink."

Epilogue

Loud music and sounds of laughter and dancing drift over the white gates of the fortress which Naina calls home.

"Dammit," Aditya curses under his breath as he stands outside the main gate and tries to think of a way to sneak inside. He ducks his head as Naina's uncle comes outside to greet an old friend of his and curses again.

It is the day of the *sangeet* which is a traditional ceremony in Hindu culture, which takes place after the engagement, but before the marriage. The groom is not allowed to participate in this ceremony and has to miss the chance of seeing his bride-to-be dressed up or to laugh and dance to cheesy marriage songs.

He is a 29 year-old healthy male with an above average intelligence and a successful career who hasn't seen or talked properly to the love of his life for five whole days. It is some stupid condition of her family that the bride and the groom cannot meet for the interim between the engagement ceremony and marriage. No doubt, cooked up by these two sisters of hers to make him suffer.

How could he have ever thought them to be cute?

He is angry, annoyed, irritated, frustrated and has an irrational urge to just storm in there, pick Naina up, throw her over his shoulder and elope. To Antarctica.

Then, as though they know that he is thinking of them, Ria and Manya ring his cell.

"Hey-lo, *jeeja ji*," Ria says in such a bright voice that it hurts his ears.

"How is my dear brother-in-law holding up?" Manya asks in a similar cheerful tone.

"Manya, I have a question," Aditya interrupts.

"Sure."

"Do I get more time in prison for murdering a police officer?"

They laugh and despite himself, he smiles. It is like hearing bells ring.

"We're having *so* much fun," Ria says.

"Exactly," Manya puts in. "And guess what? Naina is sitting right next to me. And guess what? One of your friends is sitting here."

His body chills. "What are my friends doing there?"

"Well, they turned up an hour earlier, dressed in sarees and clapping their hands, behaving like eunuchs and begging to let them in. Mom agreed."

Aditya groans and both of them laugh again.

"Don't worry," Manya chirps, "we were just kidding."

"About one of them hitting on with her?"

"No, about them being dressed in sarees. They look dashing. Tell me, who all among them are single?"

"They are dishonourable, dishonest and lecherous men," Aditya lectures. "Ria, if you dare flirt with any of them, I swear I would spank you myself."

"Aw, you're so cute," Ria replies and Aditya can hear the smile in her voice. "So, you want to talk to Naina?"

"Yes!" he says in a reverent whisper. "Five minutes, just five minutes. I promise I'd give you anything."

"No, don't give Naina the phone, Ria," Manya says from the background and Aditya glowers at the phone because he cannot glower at her.

"Oh, I don't know," Ria says in a thoughtful voice. "The

Shriya Garg

poor chap. Hasn't talked to her for *so* many days. Hey, Naina," she says loudly, "do you know who is on the phone right now?"

"Aditya?" Naina's voice comes from far away and pours over him like a balm.

"Yep. Wanna talk to him?"

"Yes! Ria," Naina's voice warns, "give me the phone."

"Let me think."

"Ria!" Aditya and Naina both growl at the same time and she giggles again.

"I am still thinking – hey! Don't snatch it…" There is the sound of feet shuffling and then running.

"Naina, you're going to spoil the henna on your hand," Naina's mother's admonishing voice comes over the instrument.

Ria's voice is a little breathless as she taunts Naina, "Oh, come on, get it. I am not going to give it, ouch!"

"Aditya?" Naina's voice sounds breathless too.

"Naina?" he asks stupidly.

"Yes. That was just Ria being stupid…"

"Haw, me? Stupid?" Ria shouts into the phone and Aditya winces. "We'll see who is stupid," she continues indignantly. "Ma, Dad," she calls out. "Look who Naina is talking to."

"I am going to kill her," Aditya mutters and Naina laughs.

"I got to go," she whispers unnecessarily as he can hear the whole chaos.

"Yeah. Listen, I…"

There is again the sound of the phone being snatched.

"…love you."

"Aw, I love you too, *Jiju*," Manya's voice giggles into the phone – loudly – and Aditya covers his face with his other hand.

"Manya, who are you talking to?" Naina's father asks her and Aditya nearly pulls his hair. Christ, no wonder Naina likes to interfere in others' matters; exactly like her whole family.

Before waiting for Manya to reply, Aditya ends the call. His hold on sanity seemed very weak.

Aditya sees an old uncle getting out of his car and hobbling with his cane to the main entrance of her house. An idea strikes.

* * * * *

"I hate you two," Naina says to her sisters as she goes to reoccupy her position on the piles of mattress laid to accommodate the guests. The whole living room has been cleared of all furniture and replaced with thick mattresses except for some space in the centre left clear for the dancers.

In a corner, just next to her, all the grandmothers are sitting with various kinds of musical instruments and even instruments like big spoons and tongs, which don't appear to be musical by any stretch of imagination, and singing.

Ria and Manya are seated in front of her, checking out the henna on her hands and laughing. For the occasion, Ria and Shaurya are dressed up like Naina and Aditya respectively. They've just finished their small skit in which they played Naina and Aditya's roles before talking to Aditya.

According to Naina, the play had been awful. All Shaurya and Ria had done was to look into each other's eyes and dance to songs and hug every couple of seconds. It was icky.

Of course everybody loved it. When in the second half, Ria (Naina) batted her eyelashes at the audience and Shaurya (Aditya) came running to save her from the long line of her suitors who always mysteriously end up in the hospital (some mystery), everybody laughed so hard that she could swear she felt the walls shake.

"We know," Manya replies cheerfully. "And Aditya hates us too. We know that too."

Ria chuckles at the mention of his name, "I almost feel sorry for him. Almost. But then I remember the way he'd hurt

230   *Shriya Garg*

you, that feeling vanishes." She turns to Laxmi who is decked in her finest clothes and her eyes shine. "Oh, we're going to have so much fun stealing his shoes!"

"Hey, don't forget me, you all," Vandana says, dropping her purse beside Naina and hugging her in greeting. Naina hugs her back, careful of her wet, henna-stained hands.

"Sorry I am so late, babe," Vandana says, taking a glass of juice from a passing waiter. "It is all because of my dumb principal. Oh, Laxmi!" she exclaims, looking at the young girl who looks beautiful in her pink dress. "You're lovely. Too bad your parents refused to let Naina adopt you. I would have loved to play aunt to you – Oh my God, Naina!" she exclaims again. "You're glowing."

"Well, I am getting married. I am entitled to it."

"That you are. Where are your other friends, Laxmi?"

"They are playing outside."

Vandana turns to see where she points and instead sees a bunch of Naina's older cousins and Aditya's friends laughing on one side. Her eyes widen; a lot like a hungry child's does when he sees a tray full of delicious chocolates.

"Let me introduce you to them," Naina grins and waves at them to come over.

"I hope you are aware that Aditya is going to kill you if he finds out you are here," Vandana chastises the group of young men who had become regular visitors to Naina's house.

"Don't worry," Vishesh, Aditya's best friend, replies with a smile. "It was aunty's order that we stay. To use Naina's favourite phrase, Aditya is stupid, but not suicidal. He wouldn't dare cross his mother-in-law."

There are a number of lewd jokes at Aditya's expense at which Naina merely rolls her eyes. All the twenty or so kids from her teaching class are creating chaos, running between people's legs and stepping on their feet, but she is too happy to care. Laxmi is sitting quietly next to her and Naina leans over to kiss her forehead.

A pang of sadness pierces her as she remembers the discussion with Laxmi's parents. After the accident that Laxmi had recently been through, her parents weren't willing to give her up again. That particular discussion had been up before it had even begun.

Aditya had tried to console her in the best way he could. But the pain was still there.

Sachin's laughter brings her back to the present. They are all very nice men, the best in their fields and yet very humble. They tease her good-naturedly and even help around with some of the older guests when the need arises. If only they could be less frank with her about Aditya's past conquests, Naina thinks with a sigh.

The new arrivals, comprising mainly of old uncles, aunts, grandmothers and grandfathers occasionally come over to congratulate her but for the most part, Naina stays with the rowdy group.

"Oh, come on, Naina," Vishesh says charmingly, "you have to dance at least one dance with me. Don't you want to see Aditya burning with jealousy even once?"

"Aditya may feel a little insecure sometimes," Naina replies, "but I can't imagine him burning with jealousy over me."

"Well, when I told him that you guys were here, he certainly sounded like he could strangle all four of you single-handedly," Ria puts in.

"Well, I *am* drop-dead gorgeous," Vishesh jokes. But his joke is not technically a joke, because aside from Aditya, he is one of the most handsome men Naina has ever seen.

Sachin takes hold of her forearm, so as not to spoil the henna design on her hand and wrist, and tugs at her, "Hey, princess, you got to dance with me too. That is only fair."

Her Mom comes over and twists one of Vishesh's ear in affection, "Vishesh, son, stop pestering Naina and instead go and distribute this tray of *samosas* over there."

Vishesh – the managing director of one of the biggest software firms of New Delhi and the whole of India – grimaces but gets up to do as she says. Sachin winks, immediately taking over his friend's space at Naina's feet.

"Why do men start behaving like a group of teenagers with their first crush as soon as they see a house full of beautiful women?" she asks.

"I believe," Shrey, another one of Aditya's friend answers, "it is because of all the oestrogen. It affects our testosterone."

Just then, an old man's coughing becomes audible over their laughter. "Don't worry...ahem, ahem...if you don't recognise me, Jai," an old man says loudly to Naina's father. "I am a very old friend of your father. You were still in your nappies when I used to come over to meet him, but then the Partition came and we got separated."

The man is dressed in a white *kurta-pyjama* and most of his face is covered by a heavy beard and hair. He looks at least seventy and walks with a limp. And yet, Naina gets a feeling that she has seen the face before somewhere.

"Just let me go wish the beautiful bride-to-be," he says and coughs again, balancing himself on his cane.

Her father stands there with the same expression on his face. He too has seen him somewhere, but cannot place him. Too bad her grandfather is taking a nap. He would have liked to meet his old friend.

He hobbles over to where Naina is seated but stops midway for a second as Vishesh passes him, still carrying the tray of food.

"Oye, young man," he shouts rudely to Vishesh.

Vishesh turns and points to himself, "Me?"

"Yes, you. Come over here and bring this old man something to drink."

Vishesh obliges and the man laughs loudly for no reason.

"Eccentric," Ria mutters and bends again to her task of decorating Naina's hand. Slowly, all the stares that had been fixed on him since his grand entrance turn away.

Naina smiles politely at him, still trying to place the face.

"Ooh, such a beautiful bride," the man beams at her and her smile wavers a little.

"I am sorry, uncle," she replies hesitantly, "but I seem to have forgotten you."

"Oh, do not worry, do not worry *ji*," he says heartily and wrapping both his arms around her waist, he almost picks her off the mattress. Naina not-so-subtly pulls away.

"I am a friend of your grandfather. My, but you're such a glowing bride! I am sure you are going to get an amazing husband. Wonderful husband. Boootyful husband. Heh heh!"

"Definitely bootyful," Manya says dryly.

Naina chokes back a laugh.

"Uh-yes, sir."

He pats her back once again, and, oh lord, is she imagining it or his grin is really lecherous?

"What sir-vir, eh?" he grins once again and something about that grin seems to ring a bell. "I am the age of your grandfather! No need to address me so formally. Just come here and give this old man a hug."

Another one?

He holds out his arm and now his smile is purely lascivious as he wriggles his bushy eyebrows suggestively.

"Come on, no need to be shy," he says and his eyes twinkle.

The bell intensifies into a full siren as Naina finally remembers where she has seen that face before.

Without a second's delay, she throws herself into his arms. Speaking in a low voice so that nobody else can listen, she asks, "What the *hell* do you think you're doing here?"

"Speak up, young lady," he says loudly, now rubbing her arms, behaving very much like the deaf Manoj Pandey she had introduced him to on Halloween.

"Aditya," she says in exasperation but doesn't remove her head from his neck. "If anyone sees you here…"

"Hey, I had to see to check whether you are still alive," he whispers back in his normal voice. "I would have died in an hour in this chaos."

She knows that she should be angry, but it feels too good. Reluctantly, she removes herself from his embrace.

"It was very nice meeting you," Naina says in her normal voice, and because she is feeling a little bit too happy on seeing him, she adds, "uncle".

He chuckles and then pretends to cough again, "Same here, same here. Wish your *bootiful* husband from my side, *daughter*. You don't know how lucky you are to have snatched such a *marvellous* catch."

She gives him a cross-eyed look to say that he is carrying it too far. His fake moustache twitches a little but he doesn't give in to the smile.

"I guess I better be going now," he says, standing back on his heels.

"Yeah," she replies, a little crushed.

He looks around for a second to see whether anyone's looking and then quickly leans over to give her derriere a little pat.

Naina's mouth forms an outraged 'O', but he merely winks and makes a show of picking up his cane.

"Naina," Shaurya comes bounding towards her and without thinking about it, picks up the old man's cane. "I think it is time for – hey, I have seen you somewhere."

Both men stare at each other. Shaurya has always been very sharp and something about that face alarms him. Aditya can't stop staring at Shaurya because he is dressed as him. Shaurya is wearing Aditya's favourite black tie which Naina had gifted him the previous month and which Vishesh must have smuggled out of his house. Shaurya is also sporting Aditya's hair-cut.

Aditya starts coughing loudly without removing his gaze from the black tie.

"Oh dear," Naina says and comes to his aid. "Here, uncle," she says, fanning his face vigorously, "let me see you to a chair."

"Is that supposed to be a very poor imitation of *me*?" Aditya whispers, in between his coughs.

"Don't ask," she mutters and puts an arm around his waist as a pretense of helping him walk.

"Here," Manya says, getting up, "you'll spoil your dress. That green henna would never come out. Let me make uncle sit."

"Alright," Naina says and drops his arm.

Manya leads him to a chair nearby where many other males of his age are sitting. Naina thinks he'd leave in a couple of minutes now that the mission is accomplished, but Aditya settles himself very comfortably and continues watching her.

More people start rocking on the dance floor and whenever any romantic song comes up, Ria and Manya would nudge her suggestively.

"Aw, such a pretty blush," Ria croons when Shah Rukh Khan professes his undying love to Kajol on the speakers. "How I wish Aditya could see you right now."

Naina's face feels as if it is on fire and she ducks it to avoid his stare.

Shriya Garg

"Yeah, me too," she mumbles when Ria pauses for a reply.

Sachin makes his way through the throng to offer everybody cups of coffee, and when he bows to Aditya, the latter pats his back so hard that his nose almost touches the ground.

"Nice man," he guffaws. "Very nice man. Tell me, lad, this girl…" he points towards Naina, "…a friend of yours?"

"Yes, sir," Sachin replies, grimacing as he tries to get up. "My best friend's fiancée."

"At least you're honest," he says with a snort and dismisses Sachin with a flick of his wrist.

Some cousins of Naina drag her mother and aunt to the floor and all four children hoot. Then Shaurya tries to drag Naina and receives a very ferocious glare from the eccentric old man in the audience.

"Shaurya," Vishesh says, pointing to Aditya, "don't you think you've seen him somewhere?"

Shaurya turns to see who Vishesh is talking about and his frown clears, "Yes, as a matter of fact, I have been thinking of the same thing."

There is a look of intense concentration on Vishesh's face and suddenly it vanishes. "Son of a bitch!" Vishesh breathes and then laughs. "That man!" He covers his face with his hands and laughs again.

"What are you talking about?" Shaurya demands impatiently.

"That's *Aditya*. Who else could it be?"

Both of them turn their gaze towards where Aditya is sitting but instead see just an empty chair.

"Aditya has been accused of being many things in his life," Vishesh says with a smile, "but stupid has never been one of them."

Shaurya also stops fighting his smile and turns to look at his sister, who is not even pretending to be interested in her mother's antics and scans the crowd for a particular someone who has just managed a lucky escape from the back-door. "Naina is one lucky girl." And doesn't she know it!

The Promise

By Chital Mehta

Price : Rs. 125
Pages : 240
Size : 5.0×7.75 inches
Binding : Paperback
Language : English
Subject : Fiction/Romance
ISBN : 9788183520133

About the book:

Dad says, 'Go to work' (how boring!)

Heart says, 'Have a blast' (yippee)

Dad kicks me out. What do I do now? (Lost!)

Friends are damn busy (Grrrrrrr)

I meet Pinky (It's definitely love at first sight, believe me!)

I join CAT class (whoa! I am in love)

My love life rolls on rocking (yeah, she loves me too. Great na?)

Dad is also happy (Son is finally studying. Duh!)

Rani steps in….nice girl, really cute (just a friend!)

She is my best friend but then…she says she loves me…

Oops… I kiss her (I didn't mean to…)

But I love Pinky (Do I?)

And I have made her a promise… (I can't break it)

This is me, Ajay. (Lost and confused madly in love)

Can you really measure friendship and love?

Step into Ajay's world which is filled with frolic, fun, confusions and craziness to discover the truth about friendship and love.

Beyond Love

By Ankit Uttam

Price	:	Rs. 125
Pages	:	224
Size	:	5.0×7.75 inches
Binding	:	Paperback
Language	:	English
Subject	:	Fiction/Romance
ISBN	:	9788183520126

About the book:

If you think that MITs, IIMs and IITs are the be all and end all of the every college.

THEN THINK AGAIN...

Get ready for a roller coaster ride in the coolest college of the country because this year your definitions will take an about-turn and on this highway many romantic hearts will be shattered.   Be ready to experience a war between your mind and your heart, for that four letter CUSS word...........LOVE.

Love is not always pure, sacrifice, friendship, cupid, red, saintly or simply a four letter word. Discover the darkest secrets of your heart where love deciphers into lust, betrayal, money, blasphemy, destruction, war, death, evil, myth and a question.

A tale of four and a half love stories and a hell lot of disaster which should not have happened and unfortunately it did happen.

Discover what the hell lies beneath and beyond those four letter word......LOVE?

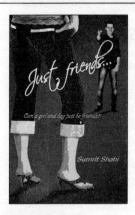

Just Friends...

By Sumrit Shahi

Price	:	Rs. 99
Pages	:	264
Size	:	5.0×7.75 inches
Binding	:	Paperback
Language	:	English
Subject	:	Fiction/Romance
ISBN	:	9788183520119

About the book:

National Bestseller

He knows everything about her, right from her favourite books to her favourite bra.

She knows everything about him, right from his favourite soccer club to his favourite x rated websites.

He will complete her English homework, even at three in the night.

She will arrange an Armani suit for him, even if it calls for flirting with ugly guys.

He has her picture in his wallet.

She has his number on speed dial.

They talk to each other all the time.

They talk about each other when they don't talk to each other.

They discuss everything from periods to playstation.

They have tasted alcohol and then thrown up...*together.*

They have bunked countless tuitions... *together.*

They can't live without each other.

       YET

They don't love each other.

They are **JUST FRIENDS...**

'Just Friends' is funny, honest, sad and straight from the heart.

—**The Indian Express**

Through his debut novel, Sumrit tries to reflect the mindset of a teenager and the relationship shared between the modern day parents and their children.

—**The Hindustan Times**

Love, Life and Ambition

By Bharat Agarwal

Price   : Rs. 99
Pages   : 240
Size   : 5.0×7.75 inches
Binding : Paperback
Language : English
Subject : Fiction/Romance
ISBN   : 9788183520102

About the book:

As a young schoolboy, Ayushman joins Scindia School in Gwalior and in no time he becomes the best student in school and icon for all.

The school ambience helps him to devote his full time to his work, and teachers always boosts him in his aim, which is to unveil Albert Einstein's Theory of Relativity, $E=mc^2$. At Scindia, his sweet classmate falls in love with him and she keeps trying to get her lascivious desires fulfilled. Similarly, Ayushman's attention too gets diverted when he sees an alluring girl by his side in a science fair, and later she becomes his devastating desire. With $E=mc^2$, love always goes parallel in their lives, though none of them knows anything about anyone's heart since the very inception of this book. What eye doesn't see and what mind doesn't know, this book has it all.

Ayushman's desire to become a next sapient Albert Einstein always has different faces. Sometimes his spirits soaring and at the other times plummeting deep below, but he always continues to strive till he brings $E=mc^2$ nearer to its final destination. After all he has to become Einstein II.

But, is it possible for someone to be next Albert Einstein? Did Albert Einstein himself ever fell in love as Ayushman? Does ever love and science go hand-in-hand?

To find out the final result, the novel has to be read as this unsaid story ends on a most unpredictable note.

Priyesh Ranjan

That's the Life Baby

By Priyesh Ranjan

Price	:	Rs. 99
Pages	:	224
Size	:	5.0×7.75 inches
Binding	:	Paperback
Language	:	English
Subject	:	Fiction/Romance
ISBN	:	9788183520003

National Bestseller

About the book:

Sixteen is sweet, Seventeen sweeter and Eighteen is the sweetest!

He thinks so.

What about Love at Eighteen? It happens, everyday! Doesn't it?

True for him!

Have a lot of girls in your life. It feels macho to have options. Girls don't need the advice. They are the wiser sex and have been playing *multi-boying* games for eons.

.....But he has three gorgeous damsels, all envious and shooting high testosterone levels.

How will you thank god if your balcony faces a girls' hostel? .....By being there 24X7? May be!

Exactly what he aims at!

Skirts lead to scandals. Don't they? Ban it or allow scandals.

He loves both, skirts and scandals.

What does he think about 'committed' tag?

You can't keep on eating the same chocolate all the time! Feels like jailed!!!

Meet Abhi. He is one of you with a devil's head! A year at Kota and his life remains no more the same. It all starts with a Bollywood-style love at first sight with Aditi. He sees, he falls, he cajoles and a little luck makes them one! Together they write new rules of dating & romance. Their amorous adventures will make you feel the passion of adolescence. But one day everything changes. How? What? Why? Answers lie in the story.

A stormy honeymoon of emotions......Get ready to laugh and cry!!!

Legally, Lovingly Yours

By Abhishek Bose

Price	:	Rs. 125
Pages	:	186
Size	:	5.0×7.75 inches
Binding	:	Paperback
Language	:	English
Subject	:	Fiction/Romance
ISBN	:	9788183520195

About the book:

Love-hate-jealousy-admiration-amity-animosity-friendship-enmity—for people in general may be only words, but for eighteen-year old Abhishek Banerjee these words turned out to be life-changing experiences over the next five years.

He harboured dreams of studying in a good college, to make new friends there, to have a girl by his side as his girlfriend, and above all, to carve out a niche for himself and leave his mark. He started realising his dreams when he got selected to study in the Animus Law School, one of the premier private law schools of the country. But, on the very first day he realised that Lady Luck was not on his side.

Could he make new friends as he had yearned for? Did he meet and get the girl he dreamt of? Was he able to make his mark? If no, then why not? If yes, then how?

Blessed with a nature endowed with patience, helpful attitude, desire for friendship, a never-say-die spirit and a never-give-in attitude, Abhishek embarks on a five-year long journey through college and on the way faces all kinds of experiences, both good and bad.

The Most Eligible Bachelor

By Satyapal Chandra

Price	:	Rs. 125
Pages	:	224
Size	:	5.0×7.75 inches
Binding	:	Paperback
Language	:	English
Subject	:	Fiction/Romance
ISBN	:	97881835208051

About the book:

Why do most love stories end with great difficulty? Why do we always claim that he or she cheated in love and caused indelible pain? Is love the name of deep understanding and mutual relationship between two souls or is it just intense desire for physical intimacy? Why does the first love invariably mean sacrifice which is against social and Nature's laws? Why don't people get selfless love in return to their selfless love for one? Why don't people again embark on the journey of love after getting cheated once?

This is an inspiring story of a self-made entrepreneur, who reaches the heights of success after confronting adversity at every step on the journey through recession, unemployment and religious discrimination; a journey through which he loses everything including his love, his best friend and his only mentor and motivator. But do these kill his spirit or his aim in life? Read this story to find answers to this and many other questions.

Let's Get Committed

By Smita Kaushik and Utkarsh Roy

Price	:	Rs. 125
Pages	:	240
Size	:	5.0×7.75 inches
Binding	:	Paperback
Language	:	English
Subject	:	Fiction/Romance
ISBN	:	9788183520157

About the book:

Hierarchy of modern age love:

Orkut > Chatting > Phone > CCD > Movies

Apurv and Radhika get committed. They try to adjust to their new marital status committed by proving the equation 1+1=1.

~ Facebook status = In a relationship…Orkut status: committed.

~ In a given area, low population density implies hands together & lesser, lips and cheeks.

~ 1st testimonial from him/her…scrapbook full of sweetheart/love.

~ Desktop wallpaper = "C:\my pictures\my.sweetheart.jpg"

This stage relates to the fact that even after liking each other, they just experiment with the concept of being together and not because of love…just in hope that they might (if it's written) fall in it.

Being a hottie, Radhika initially misses the single tag and the direct and indirect benefits associated with it. Apurv tries to reinstate the feeling of love in her but fails…though partially…

Life goes on as time tests their compatibility and then suddenly destiny shows its darker side…

Radhika is gone…

What happens next….

If it's love, will it cease to exist if they are apart?

Does Apurv find a new love?